Murder in Cottonwood Springs

A Cottonwood Springs Cozy Mystery - Book 1

BY

DIANNE HARMAN

Published by: Dianne Harman

www.dianneharman.com

Interior, cover design and website by
Vivek Rajan

ISBN:

CONTENTS

ACKNOWLEDGMENTS

Welcome to the first book in the Cottonwood Springs Cozy Mystery Series. My childhood was spent in Denver and as a court-appointed conservator for my elderly grandparents, I spent a lot of time in Colorado as an adult.

I've always loved the Rocky Mountains and have thought for several years that I needed to have a series set there, and here it is! So, to all the relatives and people in Colorado who have so graciously opened your homes and hearts to me, thank you!

And to you, my readers: I value each and every one of you. I truly appreciate your continued support, your feedback, and your ideas for future books that I may write.

As always a thank you to those people who see my books from the start through publication, Connie, Vivek, and of course, Tom, my enthusiastic in-house editor.

Hope you enjoy the read!

PROLOGUE

Lucy finished washing out the mixing bowl she'd used to make her favorite chocolate peanut butter cookies and put it in the wire mesh dish rack sitting on her wooden counter. The kitchen was one of her favorite places in the Hillcrest Bed & Breakfast, with its country décor and state-of-the-art conveniences. The entire house had been designed with a rustic feel, accentuated with displays of artifacts from the local Ute Indian tribe. Most of the artifacts on display were things her parents had picked up during their travels before they'd opened the B & B.

She was looking forward to the monthly book club meeting this evening and watching her friends devour her cookies. This particular type of cookie was her absolute favorite, and she knew if she didn't stop eating them right now, none would be left for them. Feeling righteous for making such a tough decision, she grabbed one last cookie, feeling she deserved it as a reward for the time and effort she'd put into baking the cookies.

The oven timer dinged, indicating that the last batch of cookies was ready to be taken out of the oven and cooled. When she was finished, she walked down the hall to her office where her computer was located, since she wanted to see if any more guests were scheduled to check in that evening. From what she saw, it looked like the two couples who had already checked in were the only people who would be spending the night at the B & B.

When they checked in she'd given them keys to the front door, so she could lock it when she went out or to bed. She couldn't bring herself to leave the doors of the B & B unlocked. Cottonwood Springs, Colorado was a small town, but that didn't mean it didn't have its fair share of crime. People were people whether they lived in a small town or a large city. Her brother, Rich, was the local county sheriff, and the stories he'd told her had only confirmed that yes, there was a fair amount of crime in Cottonwood Springs.

She headed back to the kitchen, glad the only meal she had to prepare for them was breakfast. She used to provide dinner for the guests, but she'd learned the hard way that when people came to this part of Colorado, they wanted to spend time in the mountains. Getting back to the B & B at a certain time for dinner was simply not a priority for them.

Lucy didn't mind, because it was one less thing she had to think about, plus she didn't have to get rid of uneaten meals. She'd gotten tired of taking leftover, or rather, uneaten food, to the church in hopes they could find a use for it. There was more than enough for her to do just taking care of the paperwork involved with the B & B and making breakfast for the guests.

She reached into the cabinet and pulled out her favorite cookie jar with a large beautiful deer emblazoned on the front of it. She glanced over at the big red clock above the oven and thought, *I wonder where Henri is?* He'd been gone a lot recently, often not returning to the B & B until late at night. He usually said something about how time had gotten away from him or something equally dismissive.

As she carefully placed the cooled cookies in the jar, she began to worry. *Maybe I should start paying more attention to him*, she thought. *He's seemed so distant lately.* Her mind began to wander, and she wondered if he was cheating on her. Maybe he'd met some young thing and was having a passionate love affair while she was at the B & B making chocolate peanut butter cookies.

The more she thought about it, the more she decided it was definitely a possibility. It would explain the distance that she felt had developed between the two of them. She couldn't remember the last time they'd made love. More often than not he found some reason to be away from the B & B once he'd finished his work for the day.

Lucy looked down at her clothes and sighed deeply. She hated to admit it, but she looked frumpy. There was no other word for it. She'd gotten used to wearing comfortable clothes, clothing that was functional. Certainly the clothing she had on was not going to appeal to a man. There was nothing feminine or sexy about baggy, worn-out blue jeans and large faded tee shirts or sweat shirts if it was a cold day. Maybe that was part of the problem with Henri. She'd definitely let herself go over the last few years when it came to wearing attractive clothes.

She set the cookie jar on the counter and headed towards her room in the back of the B & B to change clothes. *When Henri gets home tonight, I'll have a talk with him*, she decided. It was time to do something about their relationship. Even if she started wearing more attractive clothes and fixed herself up, she wasn't sure that was going to cure the problem. She knew he wasn't thrilled with running the B & B with her. He hadn't really wanted to come to the United States to be with her. Maybe he regretted the decision he'd made long ago.

Lucy remembered how romantic it had been when she'd met him. She was spending a college semester in France, and he'd begged her to stay. She was seriously considering it, but when her parents were killed in a terrible auto accident on an icy mountain road, staying was not an option. She had to return to Cottonwood Springs, take over the B & B, and become a stand-in parent for her younger brother. France was no longer an option.

She knew the only reason Henri had come to the United States was because he'd loved her and wanted to marry her. After several years, she'd become aware that Henri didn't like his role as the handyman for the B & B. She wasn't sure if it was taking orders from her, being somewhere he didn't want to be, or maybe both. In any case, in the last few years he'd become withdrawn and sullen.

She was sorry he didn't like it in Cottonwood Springs, but what could she do about it? She loved Henri and understood that he wanted to live where he considered his true home to be, and for him that meant France. But what about her? Surely Henri didn't expect her to move to France and sell the B & B.

She opened her closet door and pulled out a pale blue sweater and a reasonably new pair of jeans. She tugged off the clothes she was wearing, which were covered in flour and who knew what else, before tossing them in the clothes hamper. As she pulled the sweater over her head, she noticed a photo of Henri and her hanging on the wall that had been taken when they were in France. It felt like a lifetime ago.

They were both smiling, her chestnut-colored hair shining in the sun. They were between classes sitting on a campus bench. She thought about the way they'd been then and the way they were now. If they'd felt like that once, surely they could get those feelings back if they both tried. More than anything else, she wanted that feeling back, the feeling the happy-go-lucky couple in the photo had felt back in their college days.

She felt much better as she sat down on the end of her bed and slipped on her shoes. No matter what was going on between them, she was confident they could turn things around. He'd been madly in love with her once. After all, he'd followed her all the way to Colorado and they'd gotten married. That had to mean something. When they talked tonight she'd tell him how much she loved him, and how important their marriage was to her. For the first time in a long time, she felt hopeful about their relationship.

Lucy had a spring in her step as she headed down the hall and back towards the kitchen. She was putting the last of the cookies in the cookie jar, thinking of all the nice things she could say to Henri about improving their relationship when she heard a knock on the kitchen side door. She assumed one of the guests had forgotten their key. Smiling, she unlocked the door and turned the knob. As she opened it, some sort of substance was sprayed in her face. Her hands instinctively flew to her eyes, rubbing them to get rid of it. It burned and tears began streaming down her face.

She backed away, afraid of getting sprayed again. Lucy struggled to open her eyes, but she couldn't stand the pain. As she blindly stepped backwards to put distance between herself and the attacker who had sprayed her, she tripped, tumbling to the floor. Again she attempted to open her eyes. The pain was unbearable. The last thing she felt was a rag being held tightly over her nose and mouth that smelled foul. She tried to hold her breath, but as she fought to get away from it, she inhaled more of the fumes coming from it. It wasn't long, only a minute or so, before she was unconscious.

The intruder continued to hold the rag over Lucy's face until she stopped breathing and clearly was dead. It only took a few minutes. The murderer looked around the kitchen to make sure no clues had been left. Spying the cookie jar, the killer carefully lifted the lid with a handkerchief and took one cookie, then turned and walked out the door. The killer casually headed into the woods behind the B & B, making it look like just another guest from the B & B was out for a walk on a beautiful clear late afternoon, enjoying a cookie.

CHAPTER ONE

Brigid Barnes sighed deeply with relief as she broke down the last large cardboard box. She'd finally finished unpacking everything. The next thing she had to decide was where to put it all. She brushed her deep red hair out of her emerald green eyes. For the first time she felt like she was finally settling into her new chalet home in Cottonwood Springs, and it was a good feeling.

"That's the last of it, Jett," she said to the big Newfoundland dog lying on the loveseat in the corner. She'd never had a dog before but when the previous owners told her they had to get rid of him, she offered on the spur-of-the-moment to take him along with the house. They were thrilled with her offer and happy the big dog could stay in familiar surroundings.

It was as if there was a bond between the two of them, and she'd quickly become fast friends with the huge dog. To be honest, when she'd seen him for the first time, she was sure he was some sort of a small horse. Certainly not a dog. She'd heard of big dogs like Great Danes, but she'd never seen one in person. This big dog was really big, no, he was more than just big, he was huge, but he was really sweet and had a wonderful disposition.

She walked through the large, open kitchen as she headed to the garage to get rid of the packing box. It felt so good to finally get completely unpacked and begin to settle into her new home. On the outside it looked like a small ski chalet with its sloping roof and large, picturesque windows which looked out on the forest around her property. The home was located on the outskirts of Cottonwood Springs, so she had an uninterrupted view of the mountains and forest, including Mt. Monarch, which was at the top of the continental divide.

The killer view was part of the reason she'd been so interested in the house when the real estate agent had first told her about it. The first thing someone saw when they stepped through the front door was the amazing view, along with a sprawling great room which blended with the open concept kitchen. Down the hall were two bedrooms and her office. At the end of the hall was a bathroom with a jetted shower and a window overlooking the mountains. There was another large bathroom adjacent to her bedroom which provided a magnificent view of the forest.

Brigid was glad to be back in Colorado after more years than she cared to count in Los Angeles. In the beginning she'd enjoyed the endless things one could do there, but it wasn't long before the glitz and glamour had faded. She'd started noticing all the homeless people, the dirty streets, and the sadness in people's eyes, wondering what had become of the riches they'd expected to find there. Growing up as a small-town girl, Los Angeles had seemed larger than life in the beginning. Like so many people, she'd seen it as an escape - a place with far more opportunity than the little town of Cottonwood Springs could offer.

With time, she did find success as a book editor, but her love of the city had faded. Brigid had thought of leaving L.A., but she didn't want to start all over again. It took time to become a successful editor. When the publishing company she'd been working for suddenly went bankrupt, she realized she'd be able to keep her author clients.

She'd signed a non-competition clause with the publishing company when she was hired that would have forced her to leave the authors she did work for behind if she left the company, but since the publisher was now out of business, that no longer applied. With her work being done mainly by computer, she could live and work anywhere. About the same time the company went bankrupt, her husband divorced her. Her sister, Fiona, urged her to come home to Cottonwood Springs, and Fiona didn't have to ask her twice. For Brigid, it was the perfect time to move back to her hometown.

Brigid slowly walked into the kitchen. Earlier she'd taken all the pots, pans, plates, and silverware out of their boxes, planning to find the perfect place to put each one when she finished unpacking everything. She opened the white cabinet doors, and was wiping them out, one at a time, when she heard a knock on the front door.

Jett hopped off his loveseat, wagging his tail, and ran over to the door. "Calm down big guy," she said as she leaned down to scratch his ears. He bumped his nose affectionately against her jeaned hip. It wasn't the first time she thought perhaps she was a little crazy for having a dog that weighed more than she did. Since he wasn't growling or barking, she took that as a good sign.

She opened the door and saw a tall man who looked to be in his 40's standing there. His wavy dark hair was greying around the temples, but that was the only thing that betrayed his age. His broad chest was muscled, and he looked extremely fit. She assumed he was probably an outdoor sports enthusiast like so many of the fit guys in Colorado seemed to be. She thought he probably skied in the winter, hiked in the summer, and hunted in the fall. His suntanned skin highlighted the slight stubble growing on his chin.

"Hi," he said with a warm smile. "Welcome to Cottonwood Springs. I'm one of your neighbors and thought I'd stop by to introduce myself. I'm Linc Olson." He held out a bottle of wine. "And I come bearing gifts."

Brigid smiled at him. "People who come bearing gifts are always welcome. Please, come in." One of the perks of living in the Colorado mountains, was that the term neighbor didn't mean quite what it had back in Los Angeles. Here, there was about an acre of land surrounding each home, rather than a few feet. It left quite a bit of space between homes, and it wasn't uncommon to rarely see your neighbors. Even so, as Brigid led Linc into her great room, she couldn't help but think she wouldn't mind seeing a bit more of this neighbor now and then. She wasn't looking for a relationship, but a little male companionship would be nice.

"I'm almost finished putting things away, and this is a perfect excuse for me to take a break," she said as she took two wine glasses from the large china cabinet. She put them down on the glass table and sat down in a large brown and white plaid armchair beside the beige couch where Linc was sitting. Linc opened the bottle with a wine opener he'd brought with him and poured them each a glass.

"To you and your new home," he said as he raised his glass and looked around. "I really like what you're doing with the place, and your furniture works well with it." Jett nudged Linc's hand with his nose. "And I see you're keeping Jett. Is that a permanent arrangement?" he asked, laughing at the dog's insistent nudging.

"Yeah, the previous owners moved to a condo in Denver and couldn't take him with them. They were planning on selling him or taking him to a shelter, but I offered to take him. I met him the first time I looked at the house, and we became fast friends." She smiled at the big dog. "I've always wanted a dog, I just never expected to get one with a house, and certainly not one that's this big," she said, laughing.

"I think you'll be very happy with your decision," Linc said. "I met the previous owners a couple of times, but that was about it. Sometimes Jett would end up over in my yard when he was chasing a rabbit or a squirrel. That's the most interaction I really ever had with his owners or him, but he always seemed like such a cool dog."

"He is. They told me they bought him from a breeder in Denver who specialized in training dogs for law enforcement. I guess they thought it would make him a better guard dog," she shrugged, "although I don't know why anyone would need one out here. Seems very safe to me. I just fell in love with his fluffy face." Brigid reached down and petted Jett. In return, he licked her arm. Once she'd stopped petting him, he went to the back door and whined.

"Excuse me a moment," Brigid said. She wrapped her red flannel shirt around her as she let the dog out into the backyard, feeling the cold air come in. "So, tell me about yourself. What do you do?"

"I'm a financial advisor. Actually, I have clients all over the United States. I love the internet. No more commuting to work or dealing with an office staff," Linc said as he settled back and took a sip of his wine.

"I know the feeling. It really makes things easier, doesn't it? The internet. I love being able to work from wherever I want and wearing whatever I want. Where did you live before you moved here?"

"I lived in New York, but I got tired of the constant fast pace of life there," he said. "Sometimes when I was out late at night I found myself wondering how all the people I saw could be busy at that time of night. At some point in time I decided it was ridiculous."

"I can understand that," Brigid said. "I grew up here in Cottonwood Springs, but I moved to Los Angeles when I finished college. After my divorce and when the company I worked for went bankrupt, I decided it was time to head back home, and enjoy a slower way of life." She took a sip of her wine. Surprised by how good it was, she took another slower sip.

"You grew up here, huh? That must have been nice. I moved here after I talked to some guys in an airport security check line when I was coming back from a ski trip to Whistler, British Columbia," Linc said, smiling.

"Are you serious?" Brigid asked. She was amazed anyone would ever talk about Cottonwood Springs in general, let alone at an airport in Whistler, which was far better known than Cottonwood Springs.

"Yeah," his laugh was a low rumble. "My marriage was dead. I held no love for New York, and I was looking for a change. It sounded like a sign when I overheard these guys talking about some epic ski slopes and trails. I talked to them and when I got home I did a little research. Sounds schmaltzy, but I fell in love with the area.

The pictures on the internet were amazing, and just like that, I started looking for a place to live here.

"I found the place next door, stayed at a B & B in town for a few days until it was ready, and then moved in. The only downside is living on the outskirts of town, I haven't met many people, but that's a small price to pay for the view."

"That's crazy. I can't imagine doing something like that. Hearing about a place in passing and deciding to move there?" Brigid began to look at Linc in a completely different way than she had when she'd first met him when he'd walked through the front door as a total stranger. Obviously, he was a man who followed his intuition and did what felt right to him.

"You mean, kind of like when you moved to Los Angeles?" he raised his eyebrow as he took another drink and looked at her.

"That was a little different. I knew Los Angeles would have a lot more going on than Cottonwood Springs. You have to zoom in pretty close on a GPS before Cottonwood Springs even shows up on the map," Brigid said with a grin.

"Point taken."

They talked for a little longer, slowly working their way through the bottle of wine until a familiar scratch at the door interrupted their conversation. Brigid went to the back door to open it for Jett, and as he pushed his way into the house, Brigid saw that he was dripping wet.

"Oh, Jett, not again," Brigid said as she reached for one of the beach towels she'd started keeping on a shelf by the back door. The dog was forever going for a swim in the creek and coming back dripping wet.

"Need any help?" Linc asked as he walked into the kitchen.

"No, thanks. I've got this. He's done it to me more than once already," she complained as she grabbed for Jett. She had to hurry to dry him off before he decided he needed to shake the water off by himself. The last time he'd done that, she had to spend an hour on a ladder cleaning muddy water drops from the blades of the ceiling fan.

Linc laughed and joined her, picking up a clean towel and helping her wipe Jett down. Jett stood still, licking both of them when they got near his face. Once they were done, Brigid released Jett, and he went back to his loveseat. He circled around on it several times before finding the exact spot he wanted and then flopped down.

"It's getting late, and I really should get out of your hair," Linc said. He leaned forward in his seat and downed the last bit of wine in his glass.

"Thanks for stopping by," Brigid said. "I really appreciate you coming over here and bearing gifts. I needed a break, and it's nice to know there's a friendly face nearby."

"Brigid, if you need anything, please let me know. I'll check in with you occasionally to see if you need something done around the house. I'm fairly handy, so don't be afraid to ask for help." He stood up and began to walk towards the front door.

"Thanks. I appreciate that," she said following him. "By the way, one of my old friends, Lucy, is going to have a little coming home party for me in a couple of days. Would you like to come? It's nothing fancy. It's just a little get-together with finger foods."

"Yes, I would very much like that," he said turning back to face her. "As I said earlier, I've lived here for several months, but since all my work is done on my computer, I haven't exactly made many friends. Might be a nice opportunity for me to meet some people."

"Consider it done. It's in three days. Why don't you come here around six, and we can go together?" she asked. She wasn't going to call it a date, but it was the closest thing she'd had to one in a long time.

Linc smiled as he opened the door. "I'm looking forward to it. See you around." He walked out into the darkness with Brigid watching until he disappeared from view.

CHAPTER TWO

"Henri, I am getting tired of waiting," Joelle Dubois said as she laid on her back in her bed, still nude after making love to Henri, who was lying beside her. She stretched languidly, rubbing against him in the process.

"So am I, darling, but we must have patience. Now is not the right time. Lucy has all the money, and if I left her now I would have nothing. There would be no money to treat you like the princess you are," he said as he pulled her close, wrapping his arms around her. They snuggled down into the soft pink sheets. He sprinkled kisses along her neck as she cooed with satisfaction.

"I didn't come all the way here to Colorado from France just to be your little side fling, Henri. You promised me if I came to the United States, we could be together for a while, and then you would leave her. When we started emailing each other, you told me how much you wanted to go back home to France and be with me. It is taking far too long." Joelle propped herself up on one arm. "My patience is wearing thin, Henri."

You are not my side fling," Henri Bernard said as he pushed her dark hair away from her eyes. Trying to keep Joelle happy while he figured out what he was going to do about Lucy was a constant struggle. "I consider myself married to you more than I am to her." He pulled her down and kissed her forehead. "You are the light in my life. You complete me in every way."

Joelle pulled away from him and climbed out of bed. "Well, I don't want to wait any longer for you to keep your promises to me. I think it's time I went back to France, with or without you. I moved halfway around the world, so I could live just a few miles from you. And you know why? Because I loved you, and I believed what you told me about the two of us going to France. Now you are telling me I need to wait even longer?"

She wrapped the ivory-colored silk robe around her voluptuous body and walked over to the large wooden framed mirror above the dresser. She studied her reflection for a moment before she picked up a large paddle brush and began pulling it through her hair. "Perhaps I shall find someone else who will keep his promises to me."

"No, my pet. I promise. Only six more months. What is that compared to how long we have already waited? The time will go by before you know it. All I ask is that you give me a little more time." Henri scooted up in the bed, leaning back on the headboard. In spite of her comments a few moments earlier about finding someone else, she knew she was still very much attracted to him. His dark hair was mussed, but Joelle always thought he looked sexier that way. He'd gotten a tan from working outside so much, and although Joelle had ivory skin, she had to admit that the darker coloring suited Henri.

She used one finger to wipe away a smudge on her normally perfect eyeliner and turned to face Henri. "Perhaps the time has come for me to take a more direct approach to this problem. Waiting for you to make your move is taking far too long. Maybe I should do something about Lucy myself. Perhaps I should kill her?" she asked as she approached the bed seductively. "Boom. Problem solved."

"I hope you're kidding. No, Joelle, that is definitely not a wise thing to do," he said in a worried tone of voice. "If you were caught we could never be together. Please, let me take care of it. It won't be much longer. It probably won't even take me the full six months. I just need a little bit more time." He knew Joelle could be impulsive.

Although he loved her and didn't want to stay with Lucy any longer, he didn't want Joelle to put herself at risk by doing something rash.

Joelle turned away from him and walked over to the window, looking out on the dark street. She wasn't really sure if she trusted Henri anymore. She was torn. Maybe he really did love her and was just trying to make sure he could secure a good future for them. After all, his story never really had changed during the time they'd been together. But there was another possibility that had been floating around in her mind for quite a while and was becoming more and more insistent. She'd started to wonder if maybe Henri loved Lucy more than he did her.

She had to admit that Lucy was attractive in her own way. Lucy was a bit plain for her taste, but if she spent a little more time on herself, she could become much more attractive. Did Henri see that and think she could be prettier than Joelle? She turned around when she heard Henri getting dressed. "Are you leaving already?" she asked as feelings of jealousy coursed through her.

Henri had already pulled on his pants and was tugging his shirt over his head. "I'm afraid so, Joelle. I don't want to be too late, or Lucy may begin to get suspicious. I don't want her to find out about us, particularly when we're so close to being together forever." He sat down on the bed and began to put on his shoes. "If she found out about us now, there's a good chance she'd take everything, and I'd get nothing. I love you." He kissed her goodbye as he hurried out of the bedroom and walked towards the front door.

"I love you too, Henri," Joelle said as she followed him to the door. He turned and blew her a kiss as he stepped out the front door. She returned it, and he softly closed the door. Joelle leaned against the closed door, thinking.

"Maybe you think you need time to deal with things, Henri, but I think the time is up," she said aloud to herself. "I think I need to eliminate the one thing that's standing between us, and that one thing is Lucy."

Henri climbed into his green truck and started the engine. He was beginning to get worried. Joelle was getting impatient, and she tended to get reckless when things weren't going her way. As he backed out of her driveway and pointed his truck towards home, he knew he had his back against a wall. He couldn't stall much longer. Things were going to have to change and soon.

Lucy had been a bit of a drag in the last few years as her time and energy became completely focused on the B & B. He'd understood why she wanted to return to her hometown and take over her parents' business after they died on that icy road. And it wasn't just the business, there had also been her younger brother, Rich. But Rich was a grown man now, and Henri needed Lucy far more now than Rich did.

He had to admit he didn't enjoy their present relationship. It seemed the only time she talked to him was to tell him something that needed to be done at the B & B. Over the years, their relationship had turned more into one of employer and employee, rather than equals, a married couple.

As he drove along the dark mountain roads on his way back to the B & B, he thought about how much he'd really come to despise everything about his current way of life. When they'd first gotten together in France, Henri had loved Lucy more than life itself. She was fun-loving and vibrant, always quick with a smile. It was part of the reason he'd started seeing her even though he'd been with Joelle back then. It had been hard for him to leave Joelle, and now it was just as hard, if not harder, to have to make a choice between the two women.

Joelle was fiery and beautiful. She looked like some sort of Greek goddess that had descended from the heavens to be with him, or at least that's how he saw her, but she had another side to her. She could also be vain and selfish. Lucy was more like an earth mother, nurturing and caring. What one woman lacked, the other more than made up for it. They were like the yin and yang, light and dark, summer and winter.

Something had changed in Lucy as the years went by and she became totally immersed in her role of running the B & B. She began to smile less and less. She didn't take care of herself and barely made time for Henri unless it had something to do with the B & B. He couldn't remember the last time he'd made love to her, but at least he had Joelle.

The more he thought about it, for the first time he had to admit he really didn't love Lucy anymore. She'd become a weight around his neck, kind of an albatross, and he felt she was constantly holding him back, although from what he really couldn't say. In his heart of hearts, alone and in his car, he admitted for the first time that he'd rather be with the vivacious, passionate Joelle. He was finished with Lucy.

Henri knew that divorce was not an option. He'd end up penniless in a country he couldn't stand. No, it was time he took his future in his own hands. No more waiting for things to change on their own. They hadn't changed while he'd been in the United States, and there was nothing to make him think that things were going to change in the near future. Joelle was right, maybe the best way out of all of this was if Lucy was dead.

The more he thought about it, the more he realized it was the only way out of an untenable situation. One of the upsides if he killed Lucy was that since he was still a citizen of France, the United States couldn't extradite him for her murder. He knew an extradition treaty existed, but from the news reports he'd read about some famous people, he'd become aware that only applied when the person in France was a United States citizen. His country would protect him.

For the first time in a long time he felt hopeful about the future. With a plan beginning to brew in his mind, he pushed down on the truck's accelerator, thinking how great it would be to return to France as a single man and be with Joelle.

CHAPTER THREE

Three days later, Linc knocked on Brigid's front door and after she opened it, he said, "Are you about ready to go?" He was dressed in a hunter green shirt and dark blue jeans with a crease so sharp she wondered if he'd ironed them.

"Give me just a minute. I need to check on Jett's food and water, then I'll be ready." Linc waited by the door as Brigid walked to the kitchen. She felt like she was stalling, because she wasn't sure how she felt about Lucy and Fiona giving this party for her. She didn't like being the center of attention and she hoped her friend Lucy and her sister Fiona hadn't gone overboard with the party.

Now that the time for it had arrived, she had to admit she was even more nervous than she'd thought she would be. Her palms were slightly sweaty, and she was glad Linc hadn't tried to shake hands with her. She didn't want him to know she was shyer than she seemed. She'd tried unsuccessfully to convince Lucy she didn't need to have a welcome back party for her, but Lucy had insisted. Brigid knew her sister, Fiona, had been in on it from the start. It was hard to tell which one of them was more excited that Brigid had moved back to Cottonwood Springs. She wiped her hands on her navy-blue pencil skirt and straightened the collar of her white chambray shirt, as she glanced in the hall mirror one last time.

"Who's a good boy?" she heard Linc say as she walked back to the great room. "Yes, big old Jett's a good boy, isn't he?" Linc was kneeling down on the floor next to Jett who was on his back with his feet up in the air. Jett was rolling around as if he were a puppy getting his first belly rub. His leg started kicking as Linc found his tickle spot and started scratching.

"I see you two are getting along well," Brigid said with a laugh.

Linc stood up. "What can I say? I'm a dog guy. The bigger the better." He smiled a big, toothy grin. "By the way, Brigid, you look great."

"Thanks," she said, feeling the color rise to her cheeks. It had been a long time since she'd had a compliment from a man. "We better head over there or we'll be late, and I doubt Lucy would be happy if the guest of honor was late."

A few minutes later they pulled up outside her sister's book store, "Read It Again." It was located in the older business section of town, and was the only place one could buy books in that part of Colorado. Fiona not only sold new books, but she also bought and sold used books. Book lovers came from miles away, their cars filled with the books they'd bought and read since their last visit. There was always coffee, tea, and lemonade for people who wanted to hang around and read a book in one of the many mismatched chairs scattered throughout the store.

It was the first time Brigid had seen the book store since she'd returned to Cottonwood Springs, and she marveled at the fact that everything looked exactly as it had when she'd come back to visit a few years earlier. She looked through the large front windows and saw the same oversized chairs and small tables located just beyond the windows. Farther in were rows upon rows of new and used books. As soon as she opened the front door, Brigid inhaled the scent of old books and felt her shoulders relax. She understood why this place had become a second home to so many book lovers. The deep maroon walls added to the warm and inviting ambience.

"Hey, Brigid's here," someone said, and everyone turned to face her.

"Hi, everybody. Thanks for coming," she said. "This is my neighbor, Linc Olson." Linc smiled and waved at them.

"I'm so glad you came back," Lucy said as she hugged Brigid and greeted Linc.

"Me, too," Brigid said, and she meant it. When Fiona had first suggested she move back to Cottonwood Springs after Brigid's divorce and the bankruptcy of her publishing company, she wasn't sure she wanted to go back to the small town. She knew she wanted a change, but the more she thought about it, the more the idea appealed to her. When she'd arrived in Cottonwood Springs, she was certain she'd made the right choice. There was something comforting about being surrounded by the people you grew up with. You didn't have to try and be something you weren't, and tonight, seeing all the friendly faces only confirmed that she'd made the right move.

"Oh, it's been forever!" squealed Missy, one of Brigid's old friends. Missy still had the same curly blonde hair she'd had when they were in high school together, although now it was much longer. She was wearing a floral dress with a white background and had a very tall man in tow behind her. She gave Brigid a small hug before introducing her to him. "Brigid, I want you to meet my husband, Jordan Blair. We met in the library when we were in college. We were both studying algebra, although he was much better at it than I was."

She put her hand on his arm and said, "We got married, and a few weeks later he began attending the Seminary School of the Southwest in Austin. When he finished we were moved to several different churches in the region and only recently moved back here. He's the priest now at the Episcopal church here in Cottonwood Springs. Father Newkirk retired, and they needed a replacement. I feel so fortunate I was able to come home to Cottonwood Springs."

"Jordan, it's nice to meet you, and to both of you, congratulations. I'm glad you came back, too, Missy," Brigid said.

"We know Linc, he's been attending our church," Jordan's deep voice rumbled as he looked over at Linc. His deep voice didn't seem like it would fit him at all. He was about 6'4," and his short white blonde hair, kind eyes, and slender frame didn't give any hint of the deep timbre of his voice.

I'll bet his voice is mesmerizing when he's giving a sermon, Brigid thought.

"I have, and I've enjoyed it," Linc said. "How's the drain doing in the men's bathroom sink?"

"Much better since you took care of it, thank you again." Jordan turned to Brigid, "Linc volunteered to help fix the drain for the sink when I couldn't manage to get it to stop leaking. I'm not much of a handyman."

"It was my pleasure," Linc said. "Happy I could help."

"Brigid Barnes, I swear you look exactly the same as you did when we graduated," a familiar voice said, cutting through their conversation.

"Marissa, I'd recognize that voice anywhere. Is it really you?" Brigid asked as she turned around. The tall, leggy brunette she'd known from high school had gained about fifty pounds and had crow's feet starting to show around her eyes. She was still wearing the same square frame glasses she used to wear. The thought crossed Brigid's mind that she must really have to look to find that old style, but then again, maybe it had come back in fashion.

"Sure is, how the heck have you been?" Marissa asked.

"I'm glad to be back in Cottonwood Springs. And how have you been?"

"Oh, not too bad. I got divorced about five years ago. Other than that, things have been pretty good. I'm so happy you moved back here. We must get together soon and catch up."

The conversation of the two old friends was interrupted when Lucy began clinking a spoon against her wine glass. "Excuse me everyone, excuse me," she said in a loud voice. When the guests had quieted down, she began to speak. "I just want to say how glad I am to have Brigid back in Cottonwood Springs. I'm sure everyone knows that Brigid moved to Los Angeles after college where she became a big-time editor. Now she's made her way back home, just like the rest of us." She turned and locked eyes with her friend. "Brigid, I am so glad to have you back here. It's going to be wonderful to have coffee with you anytime I want to." She raised her glass to Brigid, "To coming home again!"

Everyone in the Read It Again book store raised their glass as well and repeated, "To coming home again!"

Brigid smiled and as she raised her glass, her eyes met Linc's. She wasn't sure she was a fan of all the attention, but it was great to get to see all of her old friends again. Everyone took a drink and then cheered.

Lucy smiled and lowered her glass, but she felt a little sad seeing her friends with their spouses. Once again Henri was out of town on business, something that had been happening more and more often lately. It would have been nice to have her own husband here to support her, or if nothing else, to at least make an appearance. Instead, she was left wondering where he was, and she was sure everyone else was as well. She'd reminded him this morning about the party, but he hadn't made any promises.

Jordan distracted Linc just before Fiona found Brigid and pulled her away to show her all the changes she'd made to the store and what she was planning on doing in the future.

"I'm thinking of adding another row of shelves over here and taking these down," Fiona began. "I wanted to have a shelf specifically set aside to highlight the idiocy I've seen happening with our elected officials, wherever they are in the United States, but Brandon talked me out of it. He said a book store is not a place for me to spout my personal political beliefs. What do you think?"

"I think Brandon is 100% correct, Fiona. I mean, people who know you well know what a warm-hearted loving person you are, even if you do have some rather different and eccentric views of how the world should be run. A lot of people who come to Read It Again might be put off by your personal views, so I think you need to keep it kind of vanilla. You don't want to alienate people who are potential customers."

"Yeah, Brigid, you're probably right. Next on my list is trying to decide where I should have a permanent set-up for the book club. I've thought about making it over by the window. I was thinking people could see in the store when we were having a meeting and might want to join us, yet something else is telling me to put it in this back corner over here."

Brigid tried to focus on what her sister was saying, but she found her eyes following Linc. She couldn't help but notice that every time she looked in his direction, he was either already looking at her or turned and their eyes would meet again. They both started smiling each time it happened, as if it was some sort of game they were playing.

"I don't blame you for looking at him," Fiona said when she realized what was going on. "He is pretty cute. Are you going to ask him out?"

"What? What are you talking about?" Brigid asked as she pulled her eyes from his once more.

"Oh, please, Brigid, don't start with me. It's plain as day to me you like him." Fiona smiled a knowing smile. She knew her sister all too well. She'd never known Brigid to not be obvious when she liked a guy. Maybe others couldn't see it as well as she could, but Fiona had always known. It was nice to see the old Brigid stepping back out into the social world.

When Fiona had gone to Los Angeles to visit her sister before her divorce, she'd acted like someone she didn't even know. That woman had been quiet and withdrawn, almost defeated. She was relieved that her condition wasn't permanent.

"Don't you think I'm a little too old for all that dating stuff?" Brigid asked. She wasn't sure she was ready for having a date and worrying about what to wear. At this point in her life, she wasn't sure she wanted to deal with all of that again.

"Uh, no, Brigid. You're not dead. That means you're young enough. Besides, it's obvious he likes you. Look at him." She smiled when she caught Linc looking over at Brigid. "I think he may have it just as bad as you do."

"Oh, Fiona," Brigid started. "I wouldn't even know what to do anymore. That ship passed me by in the night a long time ago."

"Don't be ridiculous. It's really quite simple. After all, this is the 21st century. You're acting like you're stuck in the Victorian Era. Ask him if he'd like to have dinner sometime. You can either invite him over and cook for him or you two can go out and eat. It's the modern world so you can pay or he can pay or whatever." She sighed. "Don't make a big deal out of it, Brigid. Just spend some time together and see if you two hit it off." She noticed her sister's reticence. "It really doesn't need to be complicated. It would probably be fun to have someone to fool around with. Anyway, most men your age aren't looking for anything too serious."

"Thanks, Fiona. I don't think I'm into one-night stands and let me assure you I am not living in the Victorian Era."

Fiona raised a perfectly manicured eyebrow and just looked at her.

"Okay, so I've never done anything like that, but I guess I could," Brigid said, but she was already trying to figure out how she would ask Linc to dinner. She liked him, and she definitely wanted to know more about him. Maybe a nice meal at home would help take the pressure off and feel a little more natural.

"Just think about it. That's all I'm saying," Fiona murmured. "You don't have to do it if you don't want to. Didn't you say he was your neighbor?"

"Yes, he is." Brigid had to admit her sister had a point. She could ask him over for dinner and didn't need to make a big deal of it. It would just be two neighbors getting to know each other.

Later, as the party was winding down, Brigid and Linc were in the cookbook section of the book store. He took a wild game cookbook from the shelf and they began to talk about the best way to cook venison. "I'm telling you, smoking a nice big roast is the best," he was saying.

"I don't know. My mother always used a pressure cooker and it was absolutely divine. I haven't had any venison since I left Cottonwood Springs. Los Angeles is not known for its venison," she said laughing.

"Probably so. Actually, you know what sounds really amazing to me right now?" Linc asked.

"What?"

"Ice cream," he said, patting his stomach. At that moment he looked like a big kid.

"You're on," Brigid said thinking of a hot fudge sundae. "How about you drive and I buy?"

"Sorry. I have an even better idea. I drive and I buy," he said with a smile, and she felt her stomach do a small flip. He had a killer smile, but at the same time he made her feel relaxed.

She nodded, and he extended his hand towards her. "Let's go. I bet we can slip out of here, and nobody will even know we're gone." Like two teenagers trying to get away from their parents, they started giggling as they slipped out the front door and jogged to his truck. They jumped in, and he quickly backed out as if they were making a getaway.

"I probably shouldn't have run out on my sister and Lucy, but I'll make it up to them. I thought I might lose my mind if I got hugged one more time," Brigid said, running her fingers through her hair, making sure it wasn't sticking up after their mad dash to his truck.

"I can understand that," he said. "When I was a boy, I had two aunts who loved to hug me and squeeze my cheeks. Every single time I saw them. Sometimes they did it multiple times when they got older, because they'd forgotten they'd already hugged me," Linc said with a laugh.

"That must have been torture for a young boy," Brigid teased.

He looked at her sideways and grinned, "You have no idea."

A short time later they were sitting in his truck outside of her house slowly eating hot fudge sundaes.

"I'm sorry, but we can't go in the house with ice cream. Jett begs if he smells ice cream, and he's a little big to push away. And yes, I learned that the hard way," she said, with a laugh. "The only thing that probably saved me from losing my ice cream cone to him was the fact that it was chocolate, which is not good for dogs. Otherwise I would have caved in. He made me feel so gluttonous for eating it in front of him that I didn't even enjoy it."

"I think that's probably for the best. I probably couldn't resist those big puppy dog eyes of his."

She laughed. "I know. They really are hard to resist. He also does this little huffing noise when you try to ignore him. It's like he thinks you must have missed looking at him, so he needs to get your attention."

"He's just a big hairy love bug, isn't he?" Linc asked between bites.

Brigid nodded. "It must have really been hard for his previous owners to leave him behind. Obviously, he's already wormed his way into my heart."

They ate in silence while she worked up her nerve to ask him to dinner. She didn't want to put off asking him, but she also didn't want to give him the wrong impression. The only thing she had in mind was dinner at this point. Finally, she told herself to stop thinking about it and just do it. "Why don't we have dinner some night?"

"Sounds like a great idea," he said taking a big bite of ice cream. "Your house or mine?"

"Let's do it at my house. I need to get used to my new kitchen." She finished her sundae and turned to Linc. "Thank you so much for going with me tonight. I'd probably still be stuck there if it wasn't for you. And then to end the night with a hot fudge sundae? Moving back to Cottonwood Springs seems like the best idea I've had in a long time."

"You're very welcome. Anytime." He cleared his throat. "Um, Brigid, I feel like I need to get this out of the way." She paused, unsure of what he may be getting ready to say. "I'm not looking for anything serious, but I really like you, and I'd like to get to know you better. Does that make sense?"

"Completely," she said, relieved. "I feel exactly the same way. I definitely don't want to get into anything serious for now, but I wouldn't mind seeing where this goes."

"Great," Linc said as he let out a big breath. "I'm glad we're on the same page."

"Absolutely. Well, I better head in. Thanks again for coming and for the sundae," Brigid said as she began collecting the trash from her sundae.

"Hey, don't worry about that. I'll take care of it. You don't want to have to try to hide the evidence from Jett, do you?" He took the trash from her.

"You're right, he'd probably pout, and then I'd feel awful for not giving him some. Good night Linc," she said as she climbed out of his truck.

CHAPTER FOUR

"Mike?" Lucy called out as she stuck her head outside the front door of the B & B's dark blue screen door. She wasn't looking forward to this conversation, but she knew it needed to be done.

Mike Loomis lifted his head and turned towards the door. "Need something, Lucy?"

"Would you do me a favor and come into my office? I need to talk to you, but it won't take long."

"Sure." Mike leaned the rake he'd been using against the fence and removed his gloves. He was wearing a ball cap to keep the sun out of his pale blue eyes. His beard was almost red in the sunlight, and his dirty blonde hair was curling outside the edges of his hat. It wasn't extremely hot, but he was already sweating from the yard work he'd been doing.

He went up the steps of the B & B and tried to clean his boots off on the bristle welcome mat. A few minutes later he walked back to Lucy's office. She was sitting behind her desk, straightening some papers.

"Close the door, please, and have a seat," she said, motioning to the chair across from her desk. "You know that my brother is Sheriff Rich Jennings. We're close, and he watches out for me. He also warns me if anyone I employ gets into trouble."

Mike knew where this was going. In a town this small, everyone knew everyone else's business. It was something he never could get used to. It seemed people took pride in poking their noses into places where they didn't belong, and it looked like Lucy was getting ready to be one of them. He didn't understand why people couldn't just mind their own business.

"Rich was over here the other day," Lucy continued, "and told me you'd been involved in a meth situation. I don't need to know the details, because it really doesn't matter. I told my brother you were a very hard worker and a good employee. You do what I ask of you without complaining, and you don't stop until the work is done. I really appreciate that, and Henri does, too."

He was so caught up in the fact that Lucy was talking about his personal life, Mike didn't even hear the praise she was giving him. Plus, his mind was still muddled from the hit of meth he'd done that morning before coming to work. He was very careful to never do enough to end up doing crazy stuff, just enough to help get him through the day. Anymore, it seemed like he had to do it every morning, or he couldn't function.

"I love having you around here, Mike, but I need to give you a warning. I hope you understand that I'm running a business and the reputation of the B & B, and yes, the people who work here, is very, very important to me. Even more so now with reviews on Yelp and the internet. All it takes is one bad review, and it could really affect my business.

"I simply will not allow my business to be affected because of something an employee of mine is doing. Let me make myself very clear about this. If I ever catch you high or trying to sell to one of my customers, that's it. There will be no second chances, and you will be fired immediately. I will also make sure no one else in the area gives you a job. Do you understand? I will not have that sort of thing associated with the Hillcrest Bed and Breakfast."

Figures that wimpy sheriff was behind this. Probably couldn't wait to run back to his big sister and tell her what he'd heard about me, Mike thought. *The guy's an even bigger gossip than those little old ladies who quilt together every Thursday over at the church.*

He wasn't surprised she'd called him in. Actually, he'd been waiting for Lucy to say something to him. Sheriff Jennings had stopped him on the road the previous evening and told him he'd paid a visit to his sister and made her aware Mike had been named by some snitch he'd sold some meth to. It was almost like he was proud he'd run off and tattled to Mike's employer. If he wasn't the sheriff, Mike would have punched his smug little face right then and there. Rich was very lucky he had that badge to protect himself.

"As long as you don't bring those things onto my property, it's none of my business what you do when you're not here. All I ask is that you respect my business. I have nothing against you, Mike. I think you're a hard worker and a real asset to the B & B. You help us get so much done, I'd hate to have to try to find someone to replace you, but I will if you force my hand."

Mike was nodding, but he hadn't really been listening. He was too focused on his hatred for the sheriff to hear what Lucy was saying. He was sure the sheriff was gunning for him, just looking for an excuse to put him in handcuffs. He'd probably made it his own personal mission to get Mike sent to prison.

Lucy paused for a moment to see if Mike would say anything in his defense, but when he remained silent she continued. "I think that's about it. I just wanted to make you aware of what I expected. That's all. You can go back to what you were doing." She smiled as Mike stood up and left her office.

When he was outside, all he could think about was Sheriff Jennings. He picked up the rake and tried to go back to work, but his mind was too distracted.

I just want to teach that wimp a lesson, he thought. *Maybe I'll catch him out late some night and jump him. I could probably get a couple of my friends to help.*

He decided it was time to smoke some more, so he propped the rake up against the fence and headed around back where the shed was located. Once he stepped behind the shed and into the shade it was giving off, he dipped his hand into the pocket of his jeans, retrieving his pipe and lighter. He heated up the small rock in the bottom of his pipe and took a big pull. Holding the smoke in, he decided that asking any of his friends to help him with the sheriff was too risky. Meth heads were too unpredictable. He should know, since he was one.

Mike set the pipe down to allow it to cool before sticking it back in his pocket. *Maybe if I just killed him it would be easier,* he thought. He straightened some of the tools in the shed while he continued to come up with plans for the sheriff. *Maybe I could cut his brakes? No, someone else could get hurt that way.*

He hated the sheriff, but he didn't want to hurt anyone else. He didn't picture himself as that kind of man. While he was thinking about shooting Rich, he had another thought. *I'd be stupid to do anything to the sheriff. I've watched enough cop shows to know I'd probably be one of the first suspects if anything happened to him now that there's that whole meth manufacturing investigation going on. I'd probably end up in a green jumpsuit faster than I could say, "It wasn't me."*

Mike put his pipe back in his pocket and returned to the front of the B & B to finish cleaning out the flower beds. He continued to think how he could pay back the sheriff.

There has to be some way I could make him suffer, he thought. *He has to have some sort of weakness.* He knew the sheriff wasn't married and didn't have any kids. About that time Lucy walked out the front door of the B & B and headed for her van which was parked in the driveway. *Wait, maybe that's the way to hit him where it hurts.* Mike watched Lucy climb into her van and pull away as he came up with a plan to get back at the sheriff.

If I killed Sheriff Jennings, he'd be considered to have died a hero, Mike's drug-addled mind thought. *He wouldn't suffer at all. But what if his most favorite person in all the world was murdered, right here in his jurisdiction, and under his nose? Bet it would drive him crazy. And it would serve her right for sticking her nose in someone else's business, too.*

The more he thought about the whole situation, the madder he got. Sure, he'd lose his job, but he didn't need much money to get by. The only reason he worked was so he could afford to ski during the winter season. He didn't care about much besides skiing and getting high. Everything else was just filler. He could just as easily work at one of the other B & B's in the area to make money. Mike pulled his work gloves back on and started raking as a plan began to take shape.

CHAPTER FIVE

Brigid leaned back in her black leather office chair and gently stretched her arms above her head. She felt like she'd been hunched over her desk for hours, when in reality it was probably only forty-five minutes. As an editor, she often spent a great deal of time sitting at a computer screen attempting to help authors get their novels in the best shape possible.

The hours were long, but she really enjoyed being an editor. Where else could you get paid to read great stories and help make them even better. She picked up her cell phone and began to check her email. As she was deleting yet another junk email, a message popped up from one of her authors, Rachele Peters.

Hey, I'm experiencing writer's block. Any tips? I just can't seem to break past it this time.

Brigid smiled. She considered Rachele a friend as well as a client. Her books were doing fairly well, and Brigid knew she'd been seriously working on her latest. So far Brigid was pleased with what Rachele had sent her. Not only was Rachele talented, she was one of Brigid's favorite authors to work with, because she was always willing to listen to Brigid's comments and suggestions. She never got defensive or angry. She'd worked with enough writers to know some of them really resented it when she suggested they change something. Not Rachele, though.

Have you tried taking a break for a day or so and then coming back to it? Sometimes just clearing your head for a while does wonders, Brigid typed on her cell phone and then pressed send. She went back to scrolling through her email. When her cell phone buzzed she saw it was another email message from Rachele.

Yes. Are you busy? Can I just call you?

No sooner did Brigid reply with a "sure," than her phone began to ring. She picked it up and heard Rachele let out a huge sigh.

"Oh, Brigid, thank goodness you weren't busy. I'm telling you, I just don't know what the deal is. I've never had this happen before."

"It's not uncommon," Brigid said. "Tell me what's going on."

"It's like this. No matter what I do I just end up staring at a blank screen. I've tried walking my dog, watching a movie, going to the beach, but it doesn't seem to matter. When I sit down in front of the computer, I can't come up with anything. It's driving me absolutely insane, and I feel like my deadline is hanging over me like a guillotine. It's like I've turned into one great big ball of anxiety."

Brigid understood what she was saying. This wasn't the first time one of her authors had experienced it. Sometimes a story just gets bogged down. Normally, all an author needed was a change of pace, something to happen that would inspire them. Most of the time they needed to get out of their head for a little while. They needed to stop thinking about the story and let their mind relax.

However, telling a writer not to think about their story was like telling a chef not to think about food. It was almost impossible. Brigid had met with Rachele a couple of times before she moved back to Cottonwood Springs. Rachele had always been friendly, and they had a good working relationship.

"Rachele, I have an idea. Maybe you just need a little vacation, say, a change of pace for a few days. Why don't you come to Cottonwood Springs? There isn't a lot to do here, but it's not all rush, rush, rush like Los Angeles. You can go for walks on some of the hiking trails or take a drive in the mountains. A little change of scenery never hurt anybody, and it might start those creative juices flowing again."

On the other end of the line, Rachele's eyes went wide. She was very familiar with Cottonwood Springs. She'd grown up not far from there before she ended up in prison. Brigid didn't know anything about that. Rachele had never shared that she'd been caught embezzling money at the Monarch Ski Resort when she worked there as a young woman. That was a part of her life she preferred no one knew about.

At the time she'd truly believed she wouldn't get caught. Nobody paid any attention to the books at the ski resort, so it was fairly easy to skim a little here and there. No big deal. But all that changed when Lucy got involved. For some reason, she'd decided to be a little more thorough than the previous bookkeeper, and she began running the numbers. Once she saw the discrepancies, she'd told her brother and the resort. Shortly afterwards, Rachele had been arrested, was put on trial, and when she was found guilty, she'd been sent to prison.

"You know what? That sounds like an amazing idea. Are there lots of trails where I can take a walk?" Rachele decided it was best to act as though she'd never been to Cottonwood Springs. That way there wouldn't be any questions.

"Sure, there are plenty of hiking trails and there are lots of great little shops and restaurants, as well. There's a ski resort that still has the lifts running, so you can take them up and check out the views and the wildlife, if that's your kind of thing. There's plenty here to distract you and help get your mind off of your book for a little while," Brigid said.

"Oh, Brigid, that sounds wonderful. I'm a little tight on money at the moment, though. Would you mind if I stayed with you? I can afford everything else, but paying for a room is way out of my budget," Rachele asked innocently. It was true, but she also didn't want to bring any attention to herself by staying at a B & B in town where someone might recognize her.

Rachele may have been from a couple of towns over and gone to a different school, but that didn't mean much. When she'd been caught embezzling, her face had been all over the local news. She began to type furiously on her computer, looking up airline tickets and other expenses, like a rental car. She wasn't going to miss this opportunity. No matter what it took, she was going to make this happen.

On the other end of the line, Brigid began to feel cornered. She really hadn't planned on having Rachele stay with her, but she was the one who had invited Rachele to come to Cottonwood Springs. How could she turn her down, when she was the one who'd brought it up? Brigid couldn't really blame her for wanting to skip the expense of a room. They weren't exactly cheap in resort areas like Cottonwood Springs, and it wasn't like she and Rachele hadn't gotten along. Every conversation they'd ever had was pleasant and friendly. After a short deliberation, Brigid decided having a guest for a couple of days wouldn't be all that bad. Anyway, wasn't that what guest rooms were for?

"Sure, I don't mind. You can stay with me. Maybe I can show you a few sights while you're here," Brigid said.

"Thank you so much. It just sounds wonderful. I'll book my plane ticket for two days from now. Send me your address when you get a chance. I'll be flying into Denver, so I'll just rent a car and drive over to Cottonwood Springs. I'm really looking forward to this!"

"Me, too," Brigid said, a little less enthusiastically. She felt bad, but she was already dreading Rachele's visit. For some reason, she felt like she might come to regret ever suggesting it. They both said their goodbyes and ended the call.

*****

This is going to be interesting, Rachele thought to herself. She was sitting in her office, staring at the pale blue walls. She leaned back in her chair, put her feet up on her desk, and looked around the office. *Could this be a sign? Could I really be given an opportunity to get back at Lucy after all these years? Pay her back for ruining my life? She was responsible for all those years stolen away from me, and for what? That money wasn't hers. It wasn't even her problem. If she'd just kept her nose out of my business, I wouldn't have ever been caught.* She sighed and stood up. As she paced back and forth in her small office, the thoughts whirling around in her mind began to come together.

Yes, I know it's a sign. It's a gift, although some people probably wouldn't see it that way. She chewed the corner of her thumb. *Now all I need to do is decide how I want Lucy to pay for what she did to me.*

Rachele knew her thinking probably wasn't completely rational, but how could it be? Finally, she'd have the chance to pay Lucy back for the years of her life that Rachele had lost in prison.

CHAPTER SIX

The next evening, Brigid found herself anxiously waiting for Linc to show up for dinner. When she'd invited him to dinner, she'd thought she'd feel more comfortable having dinner with him in her home rather than at a restaurant, but now she was starting to have second thoughts. Maybe Fiona had been right. Maybe she was stuck in the Victorian Era.

"What if I'm reading too much into it, Jett?" she asked as the big dog stood beside her hoping she might drop a tidbit so he could clean it up. He lifted his head as though he understood exactly what she was saying. "What if he was simply being a friendly neighbor, and I'm trying to make it into something more than it is?"

It had taken a lot of deliberation before she'd decided to make gougères as an appetizer, a forty-clove garlic chicken, a tomato tart, a garbanzo bean salad, a baguette, and for dessert, chocolate mousse. Everything had been made ahead that could be, and the house was filled with the smell of garlicky chicken. The gougères had been in the oven for fifteen minutes, so she had to find something else to fuss over. She'd already checked her hair four times in the mirror and changed her outfit twice.

Brigid wanted to look nice, but she didn't want to be too formal, either. What if he showed up in jeans, and she was wearing something dressier? She'd finally opted for a pair of black jeans and her favorite oversized pale grey sweater. It wasn't too fancy, but it was better than wearing her normal outfit of a tee shirt and jeans. She'd even debated about whether she should wear her diamond stud earrings or her hoops. She finally decided she was being ridiculous and settled on the studs.

Once she'd finished agonizing over her appearance, the house received the brunt of her nervousness. Every time she walked by the great room where she'd set the table, she'd adjust the flowers on the table or fiddle with the silverware or glasses. Something always seemed to be out of place when she looked at it.

Jett followed her into the great room and laid down on his loveseat. "What about the lighting, Jett? Do you think it's too dim? I'd like to set a nice mood, but I don't want to come off too strong. I am definitely not ready for things to go any farther than dinner."

"Woof," Jett agreed from the loveseat. Brigid stopped and looked at her new best friend. He seemed as though he was looking right at her, telling her she needed to cool it.

"You're absolute right, Jett. I'm nervous. Maybe, just maybe, I actually like this guy," she said to him. "Maybe I'd like to make a good impression on him." Jett continued to stare at her. "Okay, okay. I do like him, and I want him to like me. Is that so bad? It's just… I'd really sworn off men and dating after my divorce. It was so hard and painful. I never want to ever go through something like that again."

"Woof, woof," Jett barked, answering her.

"You are so right, Jett. It's only dinner. It's not a commitment. I need to take a deep breath and see how things go. I'm getting way too far ahead of myself here."

The doorbell rang, and Jett hopped up to go greet whoever was at the door. His tail was wagging excitedly, as if he knew Linc was on the other side. Brigid opened the door to see Linc standing there, holding a bottle of wine.

"I thought I'd bring the wine," he said, smiling his slightly lopsided grin. Looking at him, standing there in his black shirt with a dark blue tee underneath and jeans, she was struck with just how good looking he was. She'd certainly noticed it before, but this time it almost took her breath away, which made her even more nervous.

"Come in, come in," she said, holding the door open. He stepped inside, and Jett began to excitedly dance around until Linc acknowledged him.

"Hey, buddy, I'm glad to see you, too," he said. scratching behind the big dog's ears and talking gibberish to him.

Brigid laughed as she got the wine glasses out of the china cabinet and handed them to him. "If you'll pour the wine, I'll get the gougères for us."

She went into the kitchen and took the gougères out of the oven as she watched Linc and Jett interact. It was fun watching Jett be so excited to see Linc. She was learning that Jett was very discerning about the people he liked and didn't like. It was obvious Linc had made it on his friends list.

She walked back in the great room with the gougères and sat down. Linc joined her and Jett made himself comfortable next to Linc on the floor.

"What do we have here?" he asked as he picked up one of them.

"They're called gougères and served in France when people go to someone's home. Usually they're served along with champagne or kir. I've had them a couple of times, but I've never made them until tonight. I'll be curious what you think."

He finished his first one and took a second. "That's one of the best things I've ever had. It's like a bit of cheese and air. Fabulous. If the rest of the dinner is half as good as this, I will be a very satisfied man."

"Thanks. I'm happy with them. By the way, Jett must really like you, because he's giving up his favorite spot on his loveseat just so he can be near you."

"It's mutual. He's fairly intimidating at first glance, but he's like a great big kid that just wants attention."

"That's for sure," Brigid said as she took a sip of her wine. "Tell me, how did you become a financial advisor?"

"It's not really that interesting of a story. My dad and uncle started the firm before I was even born. I grew up listening to them talk about the business and thought it was fascinating. I actually ended up doing a bit of freelance accounting when I was in high school, because I was so good with numbers. I was balancing people's books and helping friend's parents balance their checkbooks.

"There never really was any question about what I was going to do when I graduated from college. From being good with numbers I graduated to the stock market, and for some reason, I had a real flair for it. I ended up getting my degree and working with my father and uncle until they retired."

"Wow. I can't imagine knowing from an early age what I would do the rest of my life. I spent most of it doing as little work as possible" Brigid said with a laugh. "If you'll excuse me, dinner is ready. Please, take a seat at the table and I'll be there in just a minute."

"I'd be happy to help," Linc said.

"Not necessary. No, actually you could light the candles. I put a lighter on the table. Thanks."

She served dinner and they spent the first few minutes in companionable silence, quietly eating. "Brigid, everything is delicious. This chicken and this garbanzo bean salad are so different. I'm really glad you suggested dinner. Now it's your turn. How did you end up becoming an editor?"

"Thank you," she beamed. "Actually, I kind of fell into it. I needed a job, and I was looking through the job listings. I responded to an ad that said they were looking for people who loved to read and found themselves correcting people's grammar. I've always had a bad habit of doing that. The job sounded like it was made for me, so I applied.

"They tested me to make sure I wasn't just saying I was a grammar nerd. I passed with flying colors. At first I started out as a copy editor, looking for mistakes. Then I quickly moved up and became an editor because I couldn't help but give the authors ideas on how I thought they could make their books better."

"Sounds like you were perfect for the job," he said. "So, you're one of those people that can't stand it when people spell things wrong?"

She laughed. "Oh yeah. Sometimes I feel like my brain is going to explode from some of the things I read on social media. I understand it's informal, but a little punctuation and capitalization goes a long way."

"I can certainly agree with that," he chuckled.

They continued to talk over dinner and when they were finished, they moved to the couch in the great room. Brigid was sitting at one end, her legs tucked up underneath her. Linc had built a fire, more for coziness than heat, although it had gotten a little cooler as the sun began to set. He was seated at the other end of the couch with Jett fast asleep, his big head laying on Linc's feet.

"If your feet get tired, just say the word. I can get him to move." Brigid said as she looked down at the big dog.

"No, he's fine." Linc leaned over to scratch Jett. "I really don't mind, and I think I like him as much as he likes me."

"He's a very likeable dog," Brigid said as she pulled her hair around to one side.

"I still think it's amazing you took him in," Linc said. "I don't know many people who would take in a dog as big as he is."

"Well, as you can tell, he's a fairly straightforward guy. As long as he has fresh water and a bowl full of food, he's happy." She looked at the dog fondly. "He's good company. I talk to him and bounce ideas off of him. And I have to admit he probably eats as much people food as he does dog food."

"I don't doubt it. Actually, he probably eats as much food as a person does, or even a horse," Linc said with a smile.

"Well, considering that I've never had a horse, I wouldn't know. But from the amount of food he eats, I imagine he could hold his own with a horse. Or at least it seems like it."

Linc stood up and walked over to the fireplace. He lifted the poker and pushed the logs around, getting them to blaze up once more. "I'm curious. What was it like growing up in Cottonwood Springs?"

"There's not a whole lot to tell. You knew everyone in your age group because even if you didn't live near them, you went to school together. Quite a few people moved away when they graduated from high school and college. But from what I've seen since I've been back in Cottonwood Springs, it looks like many of them moved back here.

"It's kind of like we can't seem to permanently stay away from the area. Everyone pretty much knows everyone, either directly or through a family member. The town's big enough that there are some people you don't know, but if you ask around you'll find out you have a mutual friend or something like that. It's kind of nice now that I'm older, but when you're a high school kid trying to get away with something, it's not an ideal situation."

"I can only imagine," he said, "but I'm having a hard time imagining you getting into trouble."

She threw her head back and laughed. "Trust me, I certainly did.

There was this guy I really liked in high school, Wade Barrett. He was kind of the bad boy in school. All the girls had a crush on him. He asked me to go swimming with him late one summer night. I didn't know he wanted to trespass and then go skinny dipping. It was definitely not one of the better nights of my life."

"Why? Did you get caught?" Linc asked.

"Unfortunately, yes. The guy who owned the land was a farmer. He saw Wade's truck parked on the side of the road and went to investigate. He found both of us and called the sheriff, who of course, called our parents. I was forbidden from seeing him ever again. And that was just part of the punishment. No television. No phone."

"And did you ever see him again?"

"Well, of course!" They both laughed, remembering how it was when you were a teenager. As soon as your parents told you not to do something, it was the first thing you wanted to do.

"I better get going," Linc said. I have to be alert in the morning. Clients don't have a very good opinion of people who are handling their money and then make mistakes with it. I'm awake long before the market's even open." He stood up, stretched, and smiled. "Dinner was fantastic, Brigid, thank you so much."

Brigid stood up and followed him toward the front door. "Not a problem, anytime."

Linc opened the door and turned around. "I guess I'll see you around," he said. His eyes fell to Brigid's lips. She could feel the weight of his gaze on her.

"Probably," she said. Before she knew what was happening, Linc's lips were on hers. Brigid opened her mouth, kissing him back. His hand cupped the back of her neck as the kiss deepened. Finally, he broke away.

"I am so sorry. That just happened. I…" he began, but she cut him off.

"Shhh. I'm glad it happened," she said, putting her finger up to his lips to stop him from talking.

He smiled slightly and said, "Good night, pretty lady and neighbor of mine. Hope to see you soon." With that he turned and walked towards his house with a lightness in his step. Brigid couldn't help but feel like the teenage girl they'd talked about earlier.

CHAPTER SEVEN

The next morning, Brigid was attempting to get some work done, but she just couldn't focus. Her dinner with Linc was still front and center in her mind, making it difficult to think about anything else. Every time she tried to concentrate on her computer screen, her mind drifted back to her evening with Linc.

She spun around in her chair and looked at Jett. "I'm getting absolutely nothing done here. Maybe if I get out of the house for a while it will help. I'll go see Fiona down at the book store. A little coffee and conversation with her is probably what I need about now." Jett didn't even lift his head from his paws.

Brigid walked down the hall to her bedroom to change. She was still in the comfortable sweatpants and tee shirt she'd pulled on when she climbed out of bed that morning. After changing into a pair of jeans and a less worn tee shirt, she pulled a brush through her hair.

"There, that should be good enough," she said as she stood in front of the full-length mirror in her bedroom. She went into the great room and grabbed her keys and purse. "Be good while I'm gone, Jett. No parties." Jett had opened his eyes when he heard his name, but once he realized she didn't really need anything, he promptly closed them again. "Oh to be a dog and be able to lay around and sleep all day," she said to herself as she locked up the house. She was starting to learn Jett's schedule and knew he wouldn't need to go out until later in the afternoon, which gave her plenty of time to go visit Fiona.

A few minutes later, Brigid pulled up in front of Read It Again. There weren't any other cars parked in front of the store, which Brigid hoped meant she'd be able to talk to her sister without any distractions. Looking through the window she saw Fiona, perfectly dressed and groomed, sitting in a large brown leather armchair near the counter, reading a book.

She grinned as she thought back to how many times she'd walked into a room, and there was Fiona, reading a book. She remembered how mad it made her parents when she'd grab a book before their weekly Sunday drive through the mountains. Fiona read the whole time they were in the car.

As Brigid opened the door to the book shop a bell rang, and a moment later Fiona said, "Hi Brigid, what are you doing here? Thought you'd be sewing curtains or something else totally domestic." She carefully placed a bookmark in her book.

"Just thought I'd come visit my sister and have a little talk. Is that so bad?" Brigid said as she smiled and sat down in the dark green recliner that was positioned across from her sister's chair.

"Well, considering you usually only want to talk when there's something on your mind, you may as well spill it. I don't know how much longer the shop will stay empty, so you better take advantage of it." Fiona picked up her coffee cup and took a sip.

"Have any more of that? I could use some."

"Sure, I just made a fresh pot. If you want cream, it's in the mini fridge. You also might want to try the new chocolate stuff that's in there. It's divine."

Brigid poured herself a cup of coffee and then sat down. She knew she wanted to talk to her sister about Linc, but she wasn't quite sure where to start. Her sister already knew she liked him. That was apparent from the chat they'd had during the party. Still, Brigid had learned a long time ago that she had to be careful about what she said to Fiona. If Fiona felt she needed to get involved, she would, and most of the time it hadn't worked out well.

Fiona had very strong opinions about pretty much anything and everything, and Brigid was the one who usually had to suffer through her tirades against whatever cause she was espousing at the moment.

"So how are things between you and your neighbor? I have to say he's pretty easy on the eyes. What's he doing with an old hag like you?" Fiona asked, teasing her older sister. They'd always talked like that to each other. They made good-natured fun of each other relentlessly, but heaven help anyone who thought they could say the same things to either one of them. It was just a game that had been going on between the two sisters since they were small children.

Brigid sighed, slightly relieved her sister seemed to read her mind. Fiona had a habit of knowing when and what Brigid needed to talk about. "Well, he came over for dinner last night," she began.

"Ohhh! Do tell. Did he spend the night?" Fiona asked as she tucked her legs up underneath her and leaned forward expectantly. She loved hearing about other people's dates. "And more importantly, I hope you're still taking birth control pills. The last thing you need is a baby."

"Speaking of which, I remember Brandon saying once how much he'd like to be a father. Let's turn the tables. When am I going to be an aunt?" Brigid asked.

"Never. I am not going to have a baby. It would ruin my figure. No thanks, that's not going to happen. I'll stick to my occasional cigarette, a good martini, and size two dresses. And you can take that to the bank."

Fiona consumed cheesy romance novels, often reading a couple a day. Brigid had always thought she liked to live vicariously through the main characters who were always single, wore the latest fashions, and were up to date on everything for women. One time she and Fiona had talked about it and Fiona had told her Cottonwood Springs wasn't much for fashion or the latest in anything, so it was her way of pretending she lived a glamorous life.

"Dinner was great, and no he did not spend the night. Jett loves him. To be honest, I was starting to wonder if he was coming over to see me or Jett. That is, until he went to leave...," she let the rest of her sentence fall away.

Fiona waited for a moment, but her sister didn't seem as though she was going to finish the sentence she'd started. "And? Come on, don't leave me hanging."

"He kissed me," Brigid said quietly. She still wasn't completely sure how she felt about it. She liked it, but at the same time she felt a little uncomfortable.

"And? Don't go all Victorian on me," Fiona asked a bit more insistently this time. Sometimes she thought her older sister was such a prude.

"And that's it, really. I kissed him back. Then he apologized for kissing me. I told him it was fine and then he left." Brigid wasn't quite sure what to think about his apology. She kissed him back, so obviously she'd liked it. Maybe it had been a long time for him just as it had been for her.

"Well, was he a good kisser?" Fiona asked, her eyebrows raised in interest.

Brigid smiled as she remembered the kiss and said, "Yeah, I'd say so."

Fiona looked at her pointedly and said, "Why do I feel like there's a 'but' in there?"

Brigid stood up and walked over to a table near the window that had a book display on it. She began straightening the pile of books. "I don't really know how I feel about dating again, Fiona. After the divorce, I told myself I wouldn't get into another relationship, that I was done with men."

"So… what? Are you telling me you're into women now? I mean you read it about all the time, but somehow I have trouble seeing you that way," her sister teased.

Brigid turned and glared at her sister. "You know that's not what I'm saying. I don't think I could emotionally handle going through something like that again." She turned back to the book display so Fiona wouldn't see the tears starting to form in her eyes. It was a touchy subject for her. Her ex-husband had really done a number on her, far more than she'd realized at the time.

He'd slowly whittled away at her confidence, until she wasn't the same person. It had taken Fiona to show her just how much she'd changed. Once she was aware of it she began the slow process of getting her self-confidence back. She wouldn't allow anyone to do something like that to her again. She doubted that she had the strength to get through it a second time.

"Brigid, what happened is in the past. You have to let it go." Fiona had joined her sister at the book table. She gently placed her hand on Brigid's shoulder. "You can't expect everything to fall apart all the time, just because it did once, and you have to keep your mind open. Maybe things will work out with Linc, and maybe they won't. That doesn't mean you stop trying, Bridge. It means if you get knocked down, you stand up, dust yourself off, and keep going. That's what life is all about. You know that."

Fiona had seen the changes that had taken place in her sister and completely understood her reluctance to become involved in an emotional relationship. Trusting someone only to have them tear you down in such a subtle way… It had to be very scary to put yourself back out there. All Fiona wanted was for her sister to find someone who made her happy and took care of her.

Brigid turned to face her sister again. "I know, and you're right.

It's just so scary being in the dating world again after all this time. I never imagined I'd be dating again after I hit age forty.

Fiona patted her arm before going over to refill her coffee cup. "Bridge, I know it's scary, but you can do this. You're a smart, strong woman. I know Bill put you through some devastating times, but the thing is, not every man is like him. Sure, everyone has their bad side, but that doesn't mean they're all as manipulative and ..."

Fiona felt her anger toward Bill rise and knew she had to force it down or she'd say something she'd regret and that might hurt Brigid. "Anyway, the point is, there are good ones out there. Who knows, maybe Linc's been hurt too, but one of you had to make the first move, and it sounds like Linc was very happy you did."

Brigid had to concede her sister's point. Linc was nothing like her ex-husband. They were poles apart. Linc was tall, outdoorsy and considerate. Bill, on the other hand, never wanted to do anything. He was happy going to the same restaurants, doing the same things, falling asleep watching TV. When Brigid suggested they do something different, he always did or said something that made her feel terrible she'd brought the subject up. No, Linc and Bill were two completely different men.

She picked up one of the books from the display table and flipped it over to read the back cover. It was about a Native American by the name of Chief Ouray. She looked over at Fiona and said, "Isn't there a town here in Colorado by that name?" She held up the book so Fiona could see what she was looking at.

Fiona looked up. "Yes, I think so. The guy who wrote the book, Ouray Smith, came to our book club once to talk about it. He wrote it because he was named after Chief Ouray, who was a relative. I didn't know a thing about him before we read the book for the book club. Apparently Chief Ouray worked hard to keep peace between the Utes and the white people who had come to settle in the area. He felt the only way to protect his people was to get along with the white men coming to live in what historically had been exclusively Ute land. He even made trips to Washington, D.C. to speak on behalf of his people. It was actually pretty fascinating."

"I didn't know that," Brigid said as she flipped through the book. She paused and looked at a few pictures in the middle of the book, reading their captions. Although she'd always liked reading about history, she'd never thought about checking out Native American history.

"Ouray Smith is a pretty intense guy. He's totally dedicated to conserving his Ute tribal heritage, so much so that he wants all their artifacts returned to their tribal council." She paused, debating whether or not to tell her sister the next part. Lucy had told her something in confidence, but after all, this was her sister. Surely it wouldn't be that big of a deal if she told Brigid. She debated for a moment, then said, "Lucy told me something, but I need you to keep it between us. I'm not sure how many people she wanted to know, and she might be angry if she found out I told you. I trust you, but still."

Brigid set the book back down and returned to her seat. "I won't say a word, Fiona, you know that." She never repeated anything her sister told her. That was one of their unwritten rules. No matter how mad they were at the other one, they would never spill the other one's secrets.

"I know. That's why I'm telling you. I trust you completely. I just don't know how Lucy would feel about it. Anyway, when Ouray Smith was here to speak to the book club, Lucy told him about her love for their culture and how her parents had bought some Ute artifacts and decorated the B & B with them. She had a lot more than I realized. I overheard her tell him she had baby boards, pottery, baskets, beadwork, really, quite a bit of stuff. She hadn't realized just how, um, how shall I say this, how dedicated Ouray Smith is to his culture.

"Turns out he's quite a fanatic when it comes to recovering artifacts that once belonged to the Ute tribe. He visited Lucy and insisted she return them to the Ute tribal council. She explained that she hadn't bought them, her parents had, and she'd always taken very good care of them, but he didn't care. Ouray told her again that she should give the artifacts back, and again she refused.

"After he left, he continued to email her and call her, almost threatening her if she didn't return them to the tribal council. You know how Lucy is. She's a very strong and independent woman, and she doesn't take that kind of thing well. She refused to give them back, but she admitted to me she was a little afraid of what this guy might do. Evidently he's still bugging her, and she regrets she ever said anything to him."

"What's Lucy going to do?" Brigid asked. "Why doesn't she just give the guy the artifacts?"

"I don't really know. It was her parent's collection. Her mother and father bought them when they were traveling. Lucy feels she has so many personal memories connected with the artifacts, she can't get rid of them. She feels she should keep them because they are a legacy to her from her parents, and now they're more hers than they are the Ute's," Fiona said.

Fiona had listened to Lucy, but she thought it would be a lot easier to simply give back the artifacts. They were just things and not worth being harassed over. Memories were something that couldn't be taken from you, even if the physical item was. Fiona wasn't that much into antiques anyway. Especially not Native American things.

"Speaking of visitors, I guess I've landed my first houseguest," Brigid mentioned as she changed the subject.

"Oh, and who's that?" Fiona asked as she pulled her cardigan around her. The seasons were starting to change, and early in the day it could be a little cool in the shop.

"It's one of the authors I work with, a woman named Rachele. She lives in Los Angeles, and she's been having some problems with 'writer's block'. I mentioned to her that a change of scenery might help her get past it and suggested Cottonwood Springs. I told her how nice and peaceful it is here, and maybe that's what she needed.

You know, get away from all the fast-paced stuff of the city. She said she had enough money to fly here and rent a car, but she'd have trouble coming up with the money for a hotel or B & B. She asked if she could stay with me. Honestly, I didn't really want her to, but since I was the one who suggested it, I couldn't really say no."

"Maybe it won't be so bad. How well do you know her?" Fiona asked, taking another sip of her coffee.

"I've met her a handful of times. We got along well enough." She paused. "I'm sure you're right. It will probably be fine. It's just, you know how I am about having people stay at my house."

"I sure do. You've never been a big fan of it. I remember that one time when I went to LA to visit you, and you went nuts because you couldn't find your hairbrush. You tried to blame it on me."

"Well, how was I supposed to know that Bill actually put something away for once?" They both laughed, remembering the incident.

"Try not to blame your houseguest if you can't find your hairbrush," Fiona teased. "I don't think that's going to get her inspired and out of your house any quicker."

"So noted," Brigid said with a smile. "Thanks for taking the time to talk with me. It was exactly what I needed. I feel a lot better now than I did when I got up this morning."

"See, I told you moving back home would be great for you. It's already turning you into a much nicer person." Fiona's large grin told Brigid she was still teasing her.

"Cute. Since when did you become a comedian?" Brigid joked. She wasn't mad at her sister, though. It was just the way they talked to each other. "Sometimes I wonder why Mom and Dad even had you. I mean, when they made perfection right off the bat, why try again? They were only setting themselves up for failure."

"Touché," Fiona said.

"How's Brandon doing?" Brigid asked, referring to her brother-in-law.

"He's doing fine. Still the manager at the Monarch Ski Resort."

"What exactly does he do out there?" Brigid asked. She couldn't imagine that being the manager at a ski resort was all that difficult, but she had no reason to feel that way.

"Well, during ski season he has to make sure all the lifts are in good working order. After all, along with snow, ski lifts are a ski resort's life blood, but he also has to keep an eye on the restaurant, the employees, things like that. There are some days he's ready to pull his hair out with all the problems it has, but he makes really good money, so that makes up for it."

"That's great, Fiona. I'm so glad for you two. It's time for me to get out of your hair. Think I'll walk down the street and check out the shops before I head home. I haven't had a chance to do that since I've been back. And Fiona, I'd love for you to come by the house now that I have everything unpacked. You saw it with me when I originally looked at the house, but now that my things are in it, it looks a lot different," Brigid said as she stood up.

Fiona walked her to the door. "I will. By the way, how are you and that big dog getting along. What's his name again?"

"Jett," Brigid answered, opening the door to the shop. "We're getting along great. He's really an awesome dog. I lucked out. I can't believe I waited this long to get one."

"I'm so happy for you, Brigid. It seems like things are really starting to fall into place for you."

"Thank you! And you know what? I think you're right," she said as she waved to Fiona and stepped out onto the sidewalk.

CHAPTER EIGHT

Ouray had just returned to his truck after spending time in the mountains on a vision quest. He'd gone up to the top of a local mountain to gain guidance from his ancestors on how to best preserve the heritage of the Ute tribe. He'd become increasingly frustrated in his attempts to conserve their artifacts and culture. He kept having dreams that he was the last one of his tribe and the tribe's heritage would be lost once he was gone. He'd felt the dreams were a sign from the spirits of his ancestors that he wasn't doing enough.

Two days earlier he'd parked his truck and climbed the mountain, taking only water and a few energy bars with him, to be used by him only in case of an emergency, but he hadn't needed them. He fasted for the entire time and allowed himself just a little water. He knew some of the younger Native Americans thought the vision quest was old-fashioned, but it was what their ancestors had done for centuries when they needed guidance or clarification about some troubling issue.

Ouray felt that just because one lived in the modern world, it didn't mean those things no longer worked. If anything, with the young people of his tribe becoming increasingly distant from their heritage, perhaps they were more necessary now than ever. It had been a long and arduous two days. At times he didn't think he would ever have a vision, but when it finally came, it was extremely clear.

His most important ancestor, Chief Ouray himself, came to him in his vision. He was dressed in traditional tribal clothing, and he explained to Ouray that the only way to keep the Ute culture alive was to bring as many cultural items as possible back onto their reservation. He was then to call in the gods to protect everything by having the tribal members take part in a sacred dance and ceremony. He told Ouray that this would protect their culture for many years to come.

Ouray had already been working hard to bring the artifacts together. He was a fervent believer that anything that had come from their culture should be returned to it. The Ute artifacts weren't items for people to hang on their walls as decorations. Each item had been touched by countless Ute natives. They were to be treasured for the stories that were held within the items, and by preserving them, he was honoring their memory as well as their story.

It was a very big undertaking, but he felt he was the man for the job. If he had been chosen for this path, then so be it. Chief Ouray's final words to Ouray were, "The ends justify the means."

Ouray started his truck, backed out of the parking spot, and began the drive home. "I will do whatever it takes to preserve our culture," he said aloud as he drove. "I will make sure that everyone knows what a wonderful man Chief Ouray was. I will pass on the story of his legacy, so that no one will ever forget him.

"I will also make sure this generation understands how important it is to safeguard our heritage. They will teach the next generation how to take care of our artifacts and land as well as preserve our stories and lessons." His greatest fear was that all his struggles would be for nothing and within just a few generations their culture and heritage would be wiped clean from memory.

He sped up as he merged onto the highway that led toward his home. He began to think about the last words Chief Ouray had said, "The ends justify the means." For some reason, his mind jumped to the woman he'd met in Cottonwood Springs, Lucy Bertrand. If what she'd told him was true, she had a fairly large collection of Ute tribal artifacts. A collection of that size should be in a museum, or at the very least, in the homes of native Utes.

Ouray's long dark hair fluttered around him as the breeze gently came in his partially rolled down window. The old truck didn't have air conditioning, but that didn't bother him. He preferred feeling the wind on his face rather than the air from the vents. He felt that the air from the vents in a car was processed just as much as food was anymore.

That's why he only went to the store when it was absolutely necessary. He preferred hunting for his food, foraging for greens, and growing whatever else he needed. It was the way his people had always lived, and he wanted to live that way, too, at least as best he could. The more he thought about it, the more he knew he had to get those Ute artifacts back from Lucy. Chief Ouray had pretty much said that during his vision quest. Ouray decided he would do whatever it took to get those pieces back where they belonged so he could fulfill the vision quest.

A moment later a thought entered his mind. *Would you? Would you do anything? Quite a bit could fall under the category of "anything." Would you be willing to kill for them? For your people and for your heritage? What if you succeed but end up in the white man's prison?*

"Yes, I would do anything to get them back," he said aloud to himself. *Maybe that's what Chief Ouray had meant,* he thought. *Maybe he was telling me to stop at nothing to get those artifacts back. After all, he was trying to preserve our way of life and culture by attempting to keep the peace during his lifetime. This isn't all that much different, is it?* "She will not stop me from getting those artifacts back!" Ouray bellowed out loud as he slammed his fist down on the steering wheel.

His anger continued to build the more he thought about Lucy's artifacts, things that rightly belonged to his tribe. Ouray recalled how often he'd tried to be reasonable with Lucy. He'd sent her numerous emails, called multiple times, and even visited her twice to ask for the artifacts to be returned to his tribe.

The last time he'd stopped by she'd threatened to call her brother, the sheriff, and get a restraining order against Ouray. The woman wouldn't budge. He wasn't afraid of a piece of paper, a restraining order, but he had to admit his efforts had fallen on deaf ears.

Continuing to talk out loud to himself as he drove down the highway, Ouray said, "She may think she's safe hiding behind her threats, but I'll kill her if I have to. If the end justifies the means, then killing her will be worth it to get back our heritage. She's just a bump in the road. Once she's out of the way, I'll be able to bring the artifacts home where they belong. With our people, on our land."

Once he'd made the decision, he was committed to it. After all, the ends would justify the means. He turned up the radio in his old truck and began to sing along with the song playing on the radio. Ironically, it was Kenny Rogers singing his famous song called The Gambler.

You've got to know when to hold 'em
Know when to fold 'em
Know when to walk away
And know when to run

Well, I'm not going to walk away or run, Ouray thought to himself, *I'm going to do what is right and has to be done.* Ouray was already planning how he would murder Lucy Bertrand and finally get the Ute native artifacts she had back where they belonged. He'd pay her one more visit, give her a chance to see the error of her ways and hand the items over. If she did it willingly, maybe he'd even make sure her name was on the exhibit at the museum. Maybe. If she refused, he'd have to go to Plan B. Satisfied with his decision, Ouray looked forward to getting home so he could to make plans for another trip to Cottonwood Springs.

CHAPTER NINE

Before Brigid knew it, the day of Rachele's visit had arrived. As the silver four-door rental car pulled into her driveway, Brigid stepped out the front door and waved to her guest. Rachele shut the engine off and climbed out, "Oh, it's so great to see you again, Brigid. Thank you so much for letting me stay with you." She hugged Brigid and looked around the outside of the house and at the landscaping. "This place is gorgeous. Maybe I need to give up writing and take up editing instead."

Brigid laughed. "No, you definitely don't want to do that. You're a very gifted author. Stay with that. Come on in. I'll help you with your bags." Rachele opened the trunk of her car and took out her suitcase and computer bag. Brigid led her to the guest room and then gave her a tour of the house. "Jett's my dog. He's outside getting some exercise right now, but I'll introduce you to him when he comes in later."

Rachele looked out the window where Jett was rolling around in the back yard. "I love dogs," she said. "One of my friends in Los Angeles has a newfie. It's a great breed."

"He's actually my first dog," Brigid said as they sat down in the great room. "Jett belonged to the previous owners of the house, but they couldn't keep him in the condominium they bought in Denver. They felt he needed a place with a yard, so when they offered him to me, I decided I'd take him. He's been really great company. I'm still learning his little quirks, but he's very easy to get along with."

"That's great. I bet it's reassuring to have a big dog like him since you're kind of isolated out here all by yourself," Rachele said offhandedly.

"I have a neighbor nearby. You can't see his house from here, but he's just up the road. Actually, we're going out to dinner in a couple of hours. You don't mind, do you?" Brigid asked.

"Of course not! Go out and have fun. I didn't come here expecting you to babysit me. I'll try to get something written."

"Thanks, and don't worry about letting Jett in. I don't want him getting confused while I'm gone, and you're here. I know he came from a trainer, so who knows what he might think. Anyway, I'd rather introduce you two when I get back." Brigid didn't think Jett would do anything, however finding a stranger in his home and his owner gone might upset him.

"Totally understandable."

"Rachele, I have plenty of food and drinks in the fridge. Please help yourself, and I want you to make yourself at home. If you get too bored, there's a small park just past my neighbor's house. It's a trailhead for a few local walking trails. If you really need some fresh air or something, you can always check one of them out. They wind around for a mile or so and then lead back to the trailhead." Brigid was quiet for a moment. "I think that's everything. Excuse me. I need to change clothes and get ready to go to dinner."

"Go, go. I'll be just fine. Don't worry about me," Rachele said as she stood up. "Anyway, I need to unpack and dig out my computer. I may drive around later to get a feel for the town."

"Sounds like a good idea. You'll have to tell me what you think about Cottonwood Springs," Brigid said.

"I will," Rachele said as she headed to the guest room while Brigid went to her bedroom.

Brigid closed the door to her bedroom and decided having a house guest wasn't such a bad thing. Even though she'd been apprehensive, it looked like it would work out just fine. It seemed that all Rachele wanted was somewhere quiet where she could focus and hopefully break through her writer's block.

She took her favorite black slacks, a peach silk shirt and a matching cardigan sweater out of her closet, put them on the bed, and went into the bathroom to shower. As she was getting ready, Brigid thought about their plans for the night. Linc was driving her to a small but well-known steak house a couple of towns away that had opened while she was in Los Angeles. It had been a long time since she'd been on an official date. It seemed that going to a restaurant certainly qualified as one.

For some reason she was really nervous about the evening. *Come on Brigid*, she thought to herself, *it will be the same as when he ate over here the other night, the only difference being you'll be out in public. You can manage that, can't you?* She certainly hoped so.

While Brigid was getting ready, Rachele was in her room doing a few local searches on her computer. She looked up the directions to the B & B that Lucy owned. It had been quite a few years since Rachele had been in Cottonwood Springs. She was determined to make Lucy pay for ruining her life, and she needed a plan in order to do that. She heard Brigid answer the door and she stepped out into the hall.

"Oh good," Brigid said when she turned around and saw her. "Rachele, this is Linc, my neighbor. Linc, this is Rachele. She's one of the writers I work with. She's been having a problem with writer's block, so I invited her to come visit me here in Cottonwood Springs to get a fresh perspective and hopefully be inspired to write something new."

"It's nice to meet you," Linc said, holding out his hand to Rachele who shook it.

"It's nice to meet you, too. You two have a good time," Rachele said as they heard a scratch at the back door.

"Sounds like Jett doesn't want to stay outside," Brigid said. She turned the knob and Jett ran in the house. He'd heard Linc's voice and wanted to greet him.

"Hey, buddy, how have you been?" Linc said as he ruffled the dog's fur. Jett licked his hand and brushed against his leg. He turned, saw Rachele, and began backing up until he was next to Brigid.

"Hello Jett. I've heard so much about you," Rachele said as she leaned over and offered Jett the back of her hand. Jett began to growl.

"Jett! What's wrong with you? I've never seen you do that," Brigid said.

Rachele leaned back, clearly hurt. "It's okay, it will probably just take a little time." She smiled at him. "I'll bet we're fast friends by the time you two are back." Jett growled again.

"Jett! That's enough. Go lie down, now!" Brigid scolded. Jett slunk off to flop onto his loveseat. "I'm so sorry, Rachele. I don't know what's gotten into him. Would you rather I put him back outside?"

"No, no. I'm sure he'll be fine. I'll just go out for a little while. Like I said, I'd like to see the town. Don't worry about it," she insisted.

"Okay. I'll see you when I get back, and if you're asleep, see you in the morning." Brigid and Linc waved as they walked out the front door.

"Have fun you two!" Rachele called as she shut the door. She sat down in the great room, waiting for Linc's car to pull away. Once she was certain they were gone, she headed to her room to grab her purse. When she re-entered the great room, Jett began to growl.

"Shhh, you'll have the house all to yourself in just a little bit. Don't be so testy," she told the dog. As she left the house, she started to feel nervous. She wasn't sure she'd be able to go through with killing Lucy. Even though her arrest and conviction had happened a long time ago, when she drove through town, it felt as though it had happened yesterday. Most of the buildings looked exactly as they had all those years ago. Some had different businesses in them, but little else had changed.

When she turned down Grove Street, Rachele caught sight of the B & B. It was starting to get dark, and the lights in the house had been turned on. She pulled into a public parking lot across the street from the B & B. There was only one other car parked in it, a black luxury sedan with dark tinted windows. It was hard to tell if anyone was sitting in the car or if it was empty. Rachele decided it didn't matter. She wasn't doing anything wrong, just parking and taking in the small-town life.

There were a couple of cars in the parking lot at the B & B and while she was looking at it she saw a figure moving in front of one of the windows. A light flipped on in the back of the B & B. As Rachele watched, she realized the person walking around the B & B was Lucy. She could tell from across the street it was her. Anger began to spread throughout her chest, up her spine, and into her head. She felt a sudden pounding in her head. All she could think of was the time she'd spent in prison because of that woman, Lucy Bertrand.

Rachele clenched her jaw. She remembered the beatings and fights she'd had when she was locked up. Her family had hardly ever visited her, then they stopped showing up at all, leaving her totally alone. She'd never seen any of them since then. Nobody cared about her, and it was all Lucy's fault. Rachele started the car and left the parking lot, knowing she needed to put as much space as she could between Lucy and her before she did something foolish, something she'd regret. She needed to think this through before she made a stupid mistake.

When she returned to Brigid's home, she went directly to her room. She felt like something had broken loose in her. She opened her laptop and clicked on the word processing document she'd saved her book on. Her fingers began to move over the keys with ease and she began writing once again. She didn't stop until her eyes were bleary, and she'd written two chapters. Grateful to be free of writer's block, she went to bed, and slept the best she had in a long time.

The following morning Rachele woke up to the smell of coffee and toasted bagels. She pulled on her cream-colored robe and stepped quietly out into the hall. Jett saw her coming down the hall and went over to Brigid where he flopped down on the floor and watched Rachele.

"Good morning," Rachele said, eyeing the dog.

"Good morning. I hope you slept well," Brigid said as she turned around. "Would you like some coffee and a bagel?"

"That sounds wonderful. Thank you," Rachele said, yawning.

As Brigid handed Rachele a plate with a toasted bagel on it she tripped over Jett. "Good grief, Jett. Why are you under my feet this morning?" she asked. Jett didn't move. "I swear it's like he's a huge boulder that just moves around the house. If he decides he's going to park himself somewhere, there's no choice but to walk around him," she said with a laugh.

"I can well imagine. He's a big boy. How old is he?" Rachele asked.

Brigid thought for a moment. "His owners said he was just a little over two years old. At least he's finished growing." She chuckled. "I'm not sure I could handle him getting any bigger."

"I can understand that," Rachele said as she spread cream cheese on her bagel. "Your home and this area seems to agree with me. After I returned from my drive last night, I was able to write two chapters."

"That's great. Where all did you go?" Brigid asked.

"Oh, I just drove around a bit. Nowhere special," she said dismissively. "I only stopped writing because I was so tired I couldn't see the screen. I plan on starting again after my shower."

"Good," Brigid said. "I have quite a bit of work to do today, so I'll be fairly busy, but there's a book club meeting tonight at my sister's book store at 6:30. I'd love for you to come as my guest. Maybe you could get some new readers. I can introduce you as an author who has another book coming out soon."

Rachele thought that was extremely nice of Brigid, but she was afraid that someone might recognize her. She couldn't exactly ask Brigid who would be attending the book club meeting. That would look suspicious. As much as she would have liked to go, she knew it was too risky. "Thanks, but I think I'll stay here and write."

"Okay, but if you change your mind, let me know," Brigid said as she picked up her cup of coffee. Jett, sensing Brigid was getting ready to leave, stood up. "I'm going to head off and get to work. Let me know if you need anything. Come on, Jett."

It wasn't until 4:00 that afternoon that Brigid saw Rachele again. She was in the kitchen and the refrigerator door was open.

"How's the writing coming along?" Brigid asked.

"Really good," she said closing the door. "I'm kind of in a flow right now. I just stopped to make a sandwich. I didn't realize how late it was."

"Are you sure you don't want to go to the book club meeting with me? I'll be leaving now as I have a dental appointment and after that I have a couple of errands I need to run. When I'm finished with those, I could swing by the house, pick you up, and take you to the book club meeting," Brigid said.

"Thanks again for the offer, but I think I better ride this creativity wave while I'm on it. Enjoy yourself and let me know how it went."

"I will. I'm going to leave Jett outside. I think maybe he needs some fresh air. He's been underfoot all day. See you later," she said as she headed out the front door.

CHAPTER TEN

After her visit to the dentist and completing a couple of errands, Brigid made her way to her sister's book store. Arriving a few minutes before the book club meeting was scheduled to start at 6:30, she opened the door to the book store and was promptly greeted by her sister.

"I'm so glad you said you'd help me. I need to straighten up the books. Would you arrange the chairs so they're all somewhat facing each other?" Fiona asked.

"Sure, do you have any snacks?" Brigid asked. "I can head to the store and get some if you don't."

"Thanks, but I talked to Lucy earlier today. She's going to bring her special chocolate peanut butter cookies tonight. I need to get tea made once everything's cleaned up and clear a space for the refreshments." Fiona rushed around, returning books to their places. "I meant to get to this earlier, but the store was busier than normal. Now that the weather is starting to cool off people are reading more."

"That's good for business," Brigid said as she moved some of the chairs around. They worked together and soon had the space cleared that was needed for the book club meeting. When they were finished, they sat down to relax while they waited for the members to arrive.

"How many people do you expect tonight?" Brigid asked.

"Twelve if I counted right. That's usually how many come to the meetings. Brandon should be here any minute." Just then, the door chime signaled that someone had entered the shop. "Speak of the devil," Fiona said.

Brandon walked in and smiled at his wife and sister-in-law. "How are you ladies?" he asked as he leaned over and kissed Fiona.

"Good, just waiting for everyone to get here," Brigid said.

"So nobody else is here right now?" he asked.

"No, why?" Fiona asked.

Brandon ran his fingers through his light brown hair and sighed. "I haven't had a chance to tell you, but I had to call Rich yesterday about Mike Loomis."

"What? What happened?" asked Fiona.

"Several guests told me he was selling meth out at the ski resort. He's really looking rough, and I noticed he was talking to himself a lot, too. I think the stuff has fried his brain. Who knows what he'll do next? I can't have that kind of thing around the resort, you know. It's bad for business, plus it's against the law, so that's why I called Rich."

"I agree with both. And you know how many people look at the reviews before they book something. One bad review…" Brigid let the thought trail off.

"I know. I feel bad since we've all pretty much grown up together but I didn't feel like I had any other choice." He sighed, obviously affected by his decision.

"Don't let it get to you, Brandon. Mike should have respected you and the resort more than that. You did the right thing. You weren't the one selling meth to the guests," Brigid said with a smile.

The door jingled again, signaling another arrival. Missy and her husband Jordan entered and waved. "Hey guys, how are you all doing?" Jordan asked.

"It was a long day but we're here now," said Fiona.

"I hear that and completely understand what you're saying," Missy said.

While they were talking, Margaret and Betty arrived. They were the oldest two members of the club, 78 and 81 respectively, but they were still spry and attended every book club meeting. They loved getting out and spending time with everyone in the group. When the weather was nice, they could often be found in the park, reading whatever book the club was reading that month.

"Evening, ladies," Brandon said to them.

"Good evening, everyone." They both waved before taking their usual spots in the most comfortable chairs the book store offered.

The next person to join them was someone Brigid didn't know, a man named Zach Thompson. He was a bit younger than the others, in his early thirties with dark blond hair that curled around his ears. He was tan and both of his ears were pierced. He smiled warmly at everyone and Brigid returned the smile. She'd heard from Fiona that he'd moved to Cottonwood Springs a few years after she had moved away. He was one of those charismatic people everyone enjoyed being around.

Three more showed up. Ben and Regina Carpenter were old friends of Brigid from school, and Margo Phillips, who was roughly Brigid's age, but was from a nearby town.

"Is Lucy not here yet?" Missy asked.

Everyone looked around but apparently Lucy hadn't arrived yet.

"Well, I wish she'd hurry up," she said. "I stopped by and talked to Lucy while I was out for a walk early this afternoon. She was just starting to make her special chocolate peanut butter cookies. Oh, my gosh," she said placing her hand on her chest. "She gave me one when I left. I have to tell you it was simply divine. I've been dreaming of having another one ever since I finished it."

A few minutes later Fiona came over to where Brigid was seated and leaned over to whisper in her ear, "I'm worried. Would you call Lucy? It's completely unlike her to be late to anything, much less when she's in charge of refreshments. Here," she said, slipping her cell phone into Brigid's hand. "Her number is in my contacts."

Brigid nodded and stood up. While everyone was catching up with each other while they waited for Lucy, she slipped into the back room and scrolled through Fiona's contacts list until she found Lucy's number. She pressed it and held the phone to her ear. She counted the rings until Lucy's voicemail picked up.

"This is Lucy. I must be busy right now, so do me a favor and leave a short message. I'll get back to you as soon as I can. Thanks!"

Brigid hung up and waited. *I'll give her a moment and try again. Maybe she can't find her phone,* Brigid thought. She couldn't count the number of times she'd thought she had her cell phone with her only to discover that she'd left it in another part of the house. After a few moments she hit redial and held the phone up to her ear. Once again, after six rings the voicemail picked up.

"This is Lucy. I must be busy right now, so do me a favor and leave a short message. I'll get back to you as soon as I can. Thanks!"

"Hi Lucy. It's Brigid. We were just worried about you, since you aren't at the book club meeting. Hope everything's okay. Let us know if you need anything."

Brigid ended the call and returned to the front of the store where the other book club members were assembled. She walked up behind Fiona and slipped the phone into her sister's hand. "No answer. I left her a voicemail. Hopefully she'll call back or show up soon," she whispered. Lucy was always on time. Even back when they were in school together, she was never tardy. It was odd for her to not at least call.

"I guess I might as well start the meeting. Keep an eye out for her, will you?" It was obvious Fiona was worried, and the last thing she wanted to do was start the meeting, but she had no choice.

"Okay everyone, we'll go ahead and get started. Lucy's probably just running late with a guest who showed up and wanted to stay at the B & B. I'm sure she'll show up soon." She kept glancing towards the door, hoping her friend would walk through it. Everyone else was looking over at the door from time to time, too.

The group began discussing the book they'd been reading. The consensus was that although they'd enjoyed it, it felt as though it was lacking something, something they couldn't quite put their finger on. An hour went by and still Lucy hadn't shown up.

"I bet Lucy will have an idea what the book needs. She's always so good at that," Betty said. Everyone agreed.

"I can't believe she hasn't shown up yet," said Margo. "Has anyone tried calling her?"

"I did earlier," Brigid said. "The call went to voicemail."

"I'll see if I can get through," Margo said, pulling her cell phone out of her purse and putting it on speaker. Everyone waited with bated breath for their friend to answer. They listened as the phone rang and went to voicemail.

They started talking about what could be taking her so long and why she hadn't bothered to call. Missy leaned over and whispered to Brigid "Do you think Lucy's all right?"

"I'm not sure," Brigid answered honestly. "I've never known her to not show up for something. She's the most organized person I've ever known."

"I'm worried," Missy began, "she mentioned something earlier…" She let her sentence trail off.

"What?" pried Brigid.

"I don't know if I should say anything. Lucy didn't say it was a secret, but that doesn't mean I should be talking about her business." Missy looked conflicted. "Maybe we should drive over to the B & B. You know, see if she's there and if she's all right."

"I agree," Brigid said. "That's better than sitting here just wondering." She stood up and walked over to Fiona. "Missy and I are going over to the B & B to check on Lucy. We've sat here worrying long enough."

Fiona nodded. "Call me and let me know what you find out," she said. Brigid put her hand on her sister's shoulder and squeezed it.

Missy whispered to Jordan what she and Brigid were going to do. He wasn't happy about them going over to the B & B by themselves in case there was a problem, but agreed that it was probably better if her friends checked on her, rather than her priest.

The two women left the book store and got into Brigid's car. It wasn't very far to the B & B. Missy spent the time chewing on her nails.

"Maybe she just forgot about the book club," Brigid said, trying to console Missy. Although she was trying to stay positive for Missy's sake, she was starting to get a bad feeling.

"She could have," Missy said, but she clearly wasn't buying it. "Looks like there are a couple of cars in the lot."

Brigid pulled into the lot and looked around the outside of the B & B. There were lights on throughout the house, giving it the appearance of someone being home. Both women got out of the car and Missy told Brigid to go to the side door that led into the kitchen. Missy knew Lucy preferred that her friends come to the side door.

The front door of the B & B was the door the guests were asked to use.

Brigid knocked on the door. They couldn't see in the window, since the blinds had been drawn. The warm yellow light from inside gave off a soft warm glow. They continued to knock several times, but no one answered.

"I'll try the door," Brigid said. Missy nodded and watched as Brigid put her hand on the knob and twisted. The door swung open. They both saw Lucy lying in the middle of the kitchen floor, not moving. Neither one of them moved or said anything. They simply stared at Lucy's body in shock.

Missy was the first to speak. "Lucy?" Her voice wavered as Brigid rushed over to her friend's side, the shock giving way to action. Her fingers reached for Lucy's wrist, hoping to find a pulse. When she couldn't find one there, she moved her fingers to Lucy's neck. Again, she felt nothing.

She looked at Missy and said in a shaky voice, "There's no pulse. Call 911." She continued to look at her friend and then realized why she hadn't been able to find a pulse. Lucy was dead.

With fumbling hands and a trembling voice, Missy called 911. When she ended the call, she called her husband, Jordan, then she and Brigid went outside to wait for Jordan and the sheriff. Since Jordan was much closer to the B & B than the sheriff, he arrived first. Missy rushed into his arms and started sobbing. He held her close for a few moments and then went over to his car and removed a book from a side door pocket.

"You know what needs to be done, Missy," Jordan said. She nodded, wiping her eyes and her sniffling nose. Brigid felt like she was in a parallel universe. It was as if she was watching her own body while she followed Jordan and Missy back into the kitchen.

"God the Father, have mercy on your servant. God the son, have mercy on your servant. God the Holy Spirit, have mercy on your servant. Holy Trinity, one God, have mercy on your servant. From all evil, from all sin, from all tribulation, good lord, deliver her." As he read, Brigid felt hot tears slide down her cheeks.

While Jordan continued reading the Ministration at the Time of Death from the Book of Common Prayer, they heard sirens blaring as they got closer to the B & B. A sheriff's car raced up and parked next to the other vehicles in the parking lot.

"Where is she?" cried Rich as he rushed out of his car. His keys and belt jangled as he hurried into the kitchen. Once he'd entered the kitchen, Sheriff Rich Jennings simply stopped and stared at the scene before him. Lying on the floor was his big sister, the one who had cared for him after their parents had died all those years ago. Now she was gone, too.

"What happened? Oh Lucy. Lucy." He fell to his knees as another sheriff's car pulled up outside. He wanted to pull her into his arms and hold her, but he knew better. He'd seen that a small rag emitting a strong pungent odor had been stuffed in her mouth. He knew she'd been murdered and realized the kitchen was a crime scene. He had to leave everything intact.

The walls of the kitchen were bathed in blue and red as the lights from emergency vehicles lit up the early evening. "I promise, Lucy. I'm going to find out who did this to you if it's the last thing I ever do." Rich was openly sobbing now, slowly losing what control he'd managed to hang onto. A deputy came to his side and helped him outside.

"We need to do our job right if we're going to find who did this, sir," he said as he guided the sheriff outside.

Deputy Davis stepped into the kitchen, "Everyone, please step outside. Need to get yer' statements, and our team needs to document the crime scene." They followed him outside and around to the front porch. Brigid saw Rich sitting in his patrol car being consoled by the deputy who had pulled him away from his sister's body.

"Wait right here," Deputy Davis said. "Need to make sure the guys showin' up know what needs to be done." Jordan nodded as Brigid and Missy stared vacantly off into space. Deputy Davis was back almost immediately. "I'm gonna' take yer' statements now."

Both women told him what happened at the book club and how everyone was worried about Lucy. They described driving over and knocking on the door. When there was no answer to their knock, they told him how Brigid had opened the door and they found Lucy lying on the floor.

Brigid had collected herself a bit by the time they were finished giving their statements. "Deputy Davis, do you know what happened to her? There was no blood, and if it wasn't for her skin coloring, I would have thought she was just asleep."

"Not certain, ma'am, but from what I smelled, my guess is chloroform. It's got a real distinct odor. Smelled it when I got close to her." He wrinkled his nose. "She was definitely murdered, I can tell ya' that."

Missy's hand flew to her mouth, and she began to sob again. "Who would want to hurt Lucy?" she cried.

"Ain't got no idea, but that's what we aim to find out," the deputy said.

"I need to call my sister," Brigid said, remembering that the book club was probably still waiting to find out what was going on. She was sure they'd heard the sirens.

"Okay," Deputy Davis said. "But don't leave yet in case I need something else from ya'." He gave her a half-hearted smile before turning and walking back to join the law enforcement people who were now swarming inside and outside the B & B.

Brigid took her cell phone out of her purse and called Fiona, who answered on the first ring. "Yes?"

She walked a few feet away from Missy and Jordan, so Missy wouldn't have to listen to the description of what they'd found. Devastated, Fiona absorbed the information and started crying as Brigid described the scene.

Would you let everyone know?" Brigid asked.

"Of course," Fiona said before she ended the call.

CHAPTER ELEVEN

After Brigid finished talking to Fiona, Missy approached her. Missy's face was lined with worry, and she was wringing her hands. "I don't know if I should tell Deputy Davis what Lucy told me," she said.

"What are you talking about?" Brigid asked in a shaky sounding voice, still lost in her own thoughts. She couldn't believe something like this could happen in Cottonwood Springs, let alone to one of her friends.

"Remember what I was telling you earlier? About Lucy being worried?" Missy asked. She picked at her fingernails as she shifted her weight from one foot to the other.

"Yes," Brigid said. "I remember you mentioning it. Why don't you tell me what it was about, and we can decide together?" Brigid was glad for the distraction, so she could get the image of her friend's lifeless face out of her mind.

"Okay," Missy said, swallowing and clearing her throat. "Lucy had a few things that were worrying her. The first one was her marriage. She told me that she and Henri hadn't been getting along lately. She said they barely talked and when they did it usually ended up in some sort of an argument.

"She was afraid he was having an affair because he was always gone. Lately his 'business trips,' as he called them, were getting longer and longer. She had no clue why he'd need to go on business trips when he was helping her run the B & B. Whenever she'd asked him about it, he'd just get defensive and leave."

"Well, every relationship has its ups and downs," Brigid said, "but it might not hurt to mention it to Deputy Davis. What else?"

"The other thing that was worrying her was this Native American guy who spoke to the book club a while back. Evidently Lucy mentioned to him that she had some Native American artifacts from the Ute tribe. After she'd told him, he became very insistent that she should turn them over to the Ute Tribal Council. You know how Lucy was about anything that had belonged to her parents. There was no way she was going to give them up. I guess he emailed her, called her, and even showed up a couple times. She told me she'd thought about getting a restraining order against him, but I'm not sure if she ever did."

"If she did, I'm sure the sheriff is aware of it, but I think I'd still bring it up." Brigid watched as the coroner and his assistant brought a body bag on a gurney out of the house and loaded it in a van. "Anything else?"

"Yes. A few months ago a couple stayed at the B & B for several days, and Lucy became good friends with them. She said the husband was a prison guard at the Colorado State Penitentiary. They'd talked about a woman Lucy testified against for embezzlement who ended up serving a sentence there."

"Really?" Brigid interrupted. "I didn't know that." It seemed Lucy had had a lot of things going on behind the scenes she didn't let very many people in on. Brigid felt like a terrible friend for not knowing any of it. But then again, what could she have done when she was thousands of miles away in Los Angeles?

"She didn't really talk about it. Once she told me she'd found out this woman was embezzling funds from the ski resort. They'd hired Lucy, through Brandon, to help them look at their books, since she's always been good with numbers, and they thought something seemed a little strange. Lucy found evidence of the embezzlement and turned it over to Rich. The woman was convicted and sent to prison.

"Anyway, the guard who stayed here knew exactly who Lucy had been talking about. He told her that the woman had gone before a parole board a while back, and it had been granted. The woman was released from prison," Missy said with a sigh. "I don't think any of that is reason enough for someone to commit murder. Lucy felt terrible for being the one who found the evidence and then had to testify against her, but what was she supposed to do? Not turn it in?" Missy's eyes were wide, as though she were desperate for answers.

"I agree, it sounds like she didn't really have much choice in the matter." A list of possible suspects was beginning to form in Brigid's mind. Apparently there were a number of people who seemed to have a grudge against Lucy, or at the very least, weren't her biggest fans. Missy was right, though, none of them seemed to have a strong enough reason to murder a person in cold blood. She knew senseless murders happened every day, but in Cottonwood Springs?

"Excuse me, ladies." A deputy approached them, looking barely old enough to be wearing a uniform. His young, kind face seemed out of place under the deputy sheriff's hat he wore. "Deputy Davis told me to tell you that you were free to go now. He'll be in touch with you if we need anything else. Do either of you need a ride?"

"No thanks," the two women said in unison. The deputy tipped his hat and returned to his colleagues. Brigid couldn't seem to shake the feeling that something was wrong. The thought of a killer walking around loose in Cottonwood Springs made her shiver. She thought things like that only happened in Los Angles, or big cities, not here in her new little hometown of Cottonwood Springs.

"Did he say you were free to go?" Jordan asked, standing up from where he'd been sitting on the porch. He hurried down the steps and joined the women on the sidewalk.

"Yes," Missy said. "I want to go home, Jordan. I don't think I'll ever be able to drive down this street again." Brigid watched as he wrapped his arm around Missy and led her to their car. He opened the door for her and waited for her to climb in before shutting it, treating her as if she was very fragile, and at the moment, she was.

As she watched them leave, Brigid thought, *I wish I had someone to console me.* At that moment, she felt more alone than she'd ever felt in her life. Although she was glad she was no longer married to her ex-husband, there was no denying not having someone around to share things with had left a bit of a void in her life. There were times when she simply wanted someone to hold her and tell her everything was going to be okay. Like now.

Brigid, Bill never did hold you and tell you everything was going to be okay. You're fantasizing. Your marriage was never like that and it never would have been like that, a little voice in her head said.

"Yeah, you're right, but I wish it had been," she answered out loud to herself.

Well, that train left the station a long time ago, Brigid, and you were never on it. There's no point in wasting your time thinking about how you wish things might have been, the little voice said. *Spend that energy thinking about what you can do about Lucy's murder.*

She wondered how Lucy had felt in that moment when she knew she was going to die? And why wasn't Henri here at the B & B? Could Henri have done it? If he had been here, she thought there was a good chance Lucy would still be alive. Wherever he was, hopefully he had a good reason for not being around. She realized she was angry at Henri, and regardless of whether that was fair or not, that's how she felt.

Brigid walked to her car and got behind the wheel. In the short time since she'd last been in it, her entire world had changed. She turned the key in the ignition and backed out into the street. She found herself heading to her sister's book store rather than home. It was as if her car had a mind of its own.

She couldn't face her house guest feeling like she did right now. She needed to be around someone who had known and loved Lucy like she did, someone who would understand what she was going through, and that person was Fiona.

Brigid pulled into a parking space directly in front of the book store and noticed that all the cars and trucks that had been there earlier were gone, with the exception of one. It was her brother-in-law's blue truck, she'd know it anywhere. When she stepped into the store, she heard her sister sobbing softly. Fiona looked up from her husband's shoulder.

"Oh, Brigid," she said tearfully, and rushed over to her sister. She pulled her into a tight hug, and Brigid felt herself losing her own composure. For the first time, she allowed the tears to come, and they flowed down her cheeks in rivers. Two strong arms circled around the sisters as Brandon joined them, comforting them as best he could. The three of them stayed that way for some time before the tears finally stopped falling.

"How could anyone do this to Lucy? Has the sheriff found out anything?" Fiona asked.

"Deputy Davis seems to be in charge of the investigation," Brigid said. "Rich just can't do it, and I can't blame him. It would be too much for him." Fiona and Brandon nodded their heads in agreement. "Davis said he smelled chloroform on Lucy and thinks that's what killed her. There was a rag that smelled of chloroform stuffed in her mouth."

"What?" exclaimed Fiona. "I didn't know that could kill somebody."

"Yeah, it can," Brandon interrupted. "I don't remember why, but I read a book once about poisons. I think we were trying to get rid of some critters at the resort. Anyway, as I remember, it said it takes all the oxygen away, so if it's held over someone's mouth long enough, it can kill them."

"That's just horrible, Fiona cried. "Who would do such a thing? Who could possibly want to kill Lucy?"

Brigid told Brandon and Fiona everything that Missy had told her earlier. Even as she told them, none of it made sense.

"You're telling us that the possible suspects, or as I read in the mysteries, the persons of interest, are Henri, Ouray Smith, and some woman?" Fiona asked incredulously. "I find that pretty hard to believe."

"I agree with you. It makes absolutely no sense to me," Brigid answered.

"There has to be something they haven't found yet," Fiona said. "I need to think about this. I won't be able to stop myself anyway, so maybe if I try to remember everything Lucy and I've talked about lately, I'll think of something that may help."

Brandon touched her arm, "Why don't you close early? We can go for a ride and just get away from everything for a little while. Might make you feel a little better," he said with a faint smile.

"That's a good idea," she said as she stood up and walked over to the door, flipping the open sign to closed. "I'll worry about all this stuff in the morning. The way I feel, I may not open tomorrow, either. I just don't know right now." She sighed deeply.

"Try not to worry too much about it," Brigid said. "And I'm sure everyone will understand if you don't open tomorrow." Looking at the two of them, Brigid was starting to feel like a fifth wheel. "I better head on home. Jett probably needs to be let out."

"If you think of anything, call me," Fiona said, as she hugged her sister one last time, both of them feeling very needy from all that had happened that evening.

"I will," Brigid promised.

"Bridge, if you don't want to stay out at your house by yourself, you can stay at our house tonight. Bring Jett, we won't mind."

"I don't think that'll be necessary, but thanks." She smiled and waved as she walked out the front door. Fiona locked it behind her and started turning the lights off in the store.

Brigid began driving home, and although she couldn't put a finger on it, something was bothering her about the evening and Lucy's death. She knew there were other pieces of a puzzle involved, she just didn't know what they were. She had the feeling it was right in front of her and she was missing it.

CHAPTER TWELVE

Brigid was distracted on the drive home. She knew she should keep her mind on her driving, but her thoughts kept drifting back to Lucy. Finding her friend lying dead on the floor had been the worst thing that had ever happened to her. She wasn't sure if she'd ever be able to close her eyes again and not see her friend's face. Unbidden tears flowed down her cheeks.

As she rounded the corner and turned down the road to her home, she saw a sheriff's car parked in her driveway. She slowed down and pulled in next to it. Sheriff Rich climbed out just as she was putting her car in park. Brigid wiped her face before climbing out, not wanting him to see that she'd been crying. If Rich could hold it together, so could she.

"What's going on?" Linc asked as he came jogging up the road and stopped next to her car. "I saw the sheriff's car through the trees and was worried. Are you okay?" He was wearing a plain tee shirt and a pair of old jeans with streaks of dirt on them. It looked as if he'd been working in the yard earlier in the day and hadn't bothered to change clothes.

"I'm fine, Linc, but Lucy Bertrand was murdered over at the B & B," she said, trying to hold herself together. Even so, her voice cracked and she had to clear her throat.

"Oh, no. I'm so sorry," Linc looked from Brigid over to the sheriff's car, his eyes wide with concern. "Do they know who did it?"

Brigid shook her head as Rich walked over to them. Brigid introduced them and said, "Why don't you two come in? I think we could all use a little company," as she waved both men towards the house. A moment later she asked, "Would either of you like something to drink? Maybe some tea or coffee?"

"Thanks, I could use a cup of coffee," Rich said as he walked towards an armchair in the corner of the great room.

"I'd love some coffee, too," Linc said as Jett exuberantly greeted him. He smiled and scratched the big dog's ears.

Brigid went into the kitchen and started the coffee before joining them. When she returned she said, "Is there something I can do for you, Rich?" she asked softly. He was pale and looked like a man who'd aged twenty years in the last few hours. Her heart broke thinking of what he must be going through.

He took a deep breath before he began to speak. "Brigid, I can't work on Lucy's case, and that's eating me up inside, but I know I wouldn't be objective. It was my sister who was murdered, so I know I'm too close to it, but it's driving me nuts. I trust my deputies, I really do. It's just that Lucy and I were so close. When our parents died, she was the one who took over the job of raising me. She went from being my sister to my mom and dad overnight. It wasn't an easy time for either one of us."

Brigid remembered Rich following his big sister around and being a pest in general when they were growing up in Cottonwood Springs. He was always threatening to tattle on them or trying to eavesdrop on their telephone conversations. If she had to guess, he was somewhere around seven years younger than his sister and a complete pain in her neck.

The aroma of freshly made coffee stopped her reverie. She excused herself and returned a few minutes later carrying a tray with the coffee and cups on it. She poured a cup for each man, then sat back, waiting for the reason Rich had come to her home to talk to her.

"Brigid, I know this may sound like an odd request, but I was wondering if you'd be willing to help my deputy, Corey Davis, with the investigation into Lucy's murder?" Rich asked.

Brigid looked at him wide-eyed. "You're kidding, Rich. Me?" Brigid was shocked. "Why me?" She took a sip of coffee to hide her confusion.

"I remember how smart you've always been. Even when I was a kid you noticed things other people didn't. Remember the school cafeteria incident? You were the one who put two and two together and found out who was breaking into it. If I knew you were helping out, and kind of looking over things, it would make me feel a lot better. I've already talked to Deputy Davis, and he's more than willing to have a little extra help."

"Rich, this is different from anything I've ever done. I mean this is serious. I wouldn't even know where to start." But as she was speaking, she remembered everything Missy had told her earlier that evening. Maybe she could be of some help. "Actually, you know what? I would be happy to help, but I can't promise you anything."

"That's all I can ask," he said, taking a big gulp of coffee. "I'm just not sure what to do with myself since I can't work on the case." His hands were shaking, and he looked defeated. Just looking at him, one knew he was probably not the same man now as the man who had gotten ready for work that morning.

"You probably just need some rest and a little time, Sheriff," Linc said as he continued to scratch Jett's ears.

"That's what one of my deputies told me," Rich said as he downed the rest of his coffee in one big gulp.

"Rich, sleep has never hurt anyone," Brigid said softly. She leaned forward and lightly touched his arm. "Go home. Get some rest."

"I think I will. Thanks for doing this for me, Brigid." He started to take his coffee cup to the kitchen, but Brigid stopped him.

"Don't worry about that, Rich. I'll take it." She took the cup from him and led him to the door.

"I'm going to call my deputy now, and I'll have him get in touch with you tomorrow. Again, thanks."

"I'll do whatever I can, Rich. You get some rest." Brigid hugged him and shut the door behind him.

As soon as the door clicked shut, Rachele entered the living room, "Is something wrong?" she asked.

Jett, who had been calmly lying at Linc's feet hopped up and hurried over to Brigid. As she moved back to the couch, Jett followed, sitting at her feet.

"One of my close friends, Lucy, who ran the local B & B, was murdered this evening. Another friend and I were the ones to find her." Brigid blinked back the tears that were threatening to fall again. "I just don't understand why someone would do such a thing. Lucy was a good woman.

"She took over her parents' B & B when they died unexpectedly, and then she raised her little brother. She always knew how to make the best out of any situation. I just can't believe she's gone," Brigid couldn't control her tears any longer and began to cry softly.

"I'm sorry for your loss, Brigid. I can't imagine how horrible it must have been to find your friend like that. She sounds like she was a wonderful person. I wish I could have met her." Rachele sighed. "Well, I was just going to get a drink of water when I saw the sheriff's car outside. I'll leave you two alone." She went into the kitchen and got a glass of water before disappearing back down the hall.

Once Rachele had left, Linc stood up and moved next to Brigid on the couch. He pulled her close, wrapping his arms around her, trying to comfort her. Brigid began to sob. She allowed herself to sink into Linc's arms, feeling safe and secure, even if only for a little while. After her tears finally slowed and she could collect her thoughts, she pulled away from him.

"Thank you," she said quietly. "I really appreciate you being here for me and checking in when you saw the sheriff's car."

"No thanks necessary, Brigid. I was worried about you. You should probably get some sleep, too." He rubbed her back gently. "I hate to ask, but do you have a gun?"

"A gun?" she asked. "No, of course not. Why would you ask something like that?"

"Because a woman was murdered tonight, and nobody knows why right now. Add to that the fact you're going to be helping the sheriff's department investigate her murder, and I think you really need one. I want you to take mine. I'll come over tomorrow morning at eight to show you how to use it safely."

"Thank you, but I don't think so. I hate guns, the NRA, all of it."

"Brigid, this isn't about politics or social beliefs or any of that stuff. This is strictly about you being safe. I want to make sure you can protect yourself if necessary. Simply stated, if you're investigating a murder, you need protection."

"You're not investigating a murder, so why do you have one?" Brigid asked. She really didn't see why the average person needed to carry a gun.

"Most people in mountain communities have them, Brigid. I have one because I'm worried some client might decide to take it out on me when the stock market's having a down day. Some people go a little crazy when it comes to their money. Kind of a 'shoot the messenger' sort of thing," he sighed. "Look, it's a real small pistol. It will fit in your purse with no problem. It's so small I carry it in my pants pocket."

"Let's see how it goes tomorrow morning. I'm not making any promises, though," Brigid said.

"Not a problem. I can work with that. Would you do me one more favor?" he asked, afraid he might be pushing his luck with her.

"What now?" Brigid asked, laughing for the first time that evening.

"Keep Jett with you. Take him with you when you leave the house."

"Why? Good grief, if I'm carrying a gun I don't exactly need a big dog, too. Seems a bit like overkill to me."

"Actually, Newfoundland dogs are known for being excellent guard dogs, even though they're really loveable and sweet. Besides, he's massive. Nobody is going to try anything with this big guy next to you." He turned and looked down at his feet, where Jett was lying. "Right, Jett?" Linc reached down and began to stroke Jett's side affectionately. The big dog rolled over on his back and began wagging his tail, thumping it on the floor.

"You don't have a dog," Brigid pointed out. "What makes you such an expert on them?"

"Well, Miss Sassy Pants," Linc said with a laugh. "If you must know, my brother has had a number of them over the years, so I'm very familiar with the breed."

"All right, you win. I'll take Jett with me whenever possible."

"Good. Go get some rest. I'm going to head home, and I'll pick you up in the morning." Linc walked over to the door. "Be ready to show those targets at the gun range who's boss."

CHAPTER THIRTEEN

The next morning, Linc showed up exactly at eight to take Brigid to the gun range. As they climbed into his truck, Linc could tell she was nervous.

"What's the problem?" he asked while he attached his seatbelt.

"I don't know if this is such a good idea," she admitted. "I am not a gun person. I'm not sure I can pull this off." She picked at some imaginary lint on her shirt.

Linc smiled and took her hand. "Brigid, it's okay. There's no pressure here. I just want to make sure you're safe at all times. How's this? If, by the end of the day, you still don't feel comfortable about the gun, you don't have to keep it with you. I don't want to force you to do something you don't want to do." Brigid looked up at him, relief spreading across her face. "But, I want you to give it an honest try, and if you feel okay with it, I want you to hang onto it until this whole thing is over. Is that fair?"

Brigid nodded, "Yes, I can go with that."

There were two sections to the gun range, an indoor one and an outdoor one. Linc chose to take her outdoors. He had a feeling the cold cinder block walls inside the building might be intimidating and claustrophobic to her. He pushed the door open and led her outdoors. It was a beautiful, crisp morning, and the fresh air felt good on Brigid's skin.

While she was against guns in general, she had to admit that what Linc had said the night before made sense. If she was going to be looking for a killer, it was probably smart to be well protected. The fact she knew she could back out if she was terrible with it made her breathe much easier.

"Okay, Brigid, this is fairly simple. First, you want to make sure you click the safety off before you try to use it." He showed her where the little button was and how to push it. "Now it's ready to fire. Pull this back, and it will load a bullet in the firing chamber." He pulled back on the top of the gun and released it. "After that, hold it up, and look down the top of the barrel. That's where the sights are. You want the two rear sights located right here to be on either side of the front sight up here," he said pointing to each part. He held the gun pointed down range at the target the whole time.

Linc fired a few rounds before handing the gun over to Brigid. "Now I'm going to put the safety back on, so you can practice holding it and aiming at the target without firing." He did and then handed it to her.

Even though the pistol was quite small, it was heavier than Brigid had anticipated, and it was cold. It struck her how easily people killed each other with such a small thing. It was a bit terrifying and humbling at the same time.

"This really feels strange to me, Linc," she admitted.

"Give it time. I felt the same way, too, until I got used to it. As long as you're smart and responsible, and you are, there's no reason to be afraid of it." Linc smiled encouragingly, and Brigid forced herself to relax. She followed Linc's instructions and held the gun up. As she looked down the barrel and focused on the sights she felt her confidence waver.

"Don't think too much about it. Before you pull the trigger, take a deep breath, and then hold it. That will help you steady yourself," Linc instructed.

She clicked off the safety, took a long, steadying breath and then held it before pulling the trigger. The recoil of the gun surprised her. It had much more of a kick than she thought it would. Her first shot missed the target completely.

"That's okay. Just relax." Linc moved closer. "Here let me show you." He moved behind Brigid, wrapping his arms around her. He took her hands and held the gun up. "Look down the sights," he said softly, his warm breath tickling her ear. "You're the boss here. Always remember that. You're calm and in control." He adjusted her hands slightly "Pull the trigger with a gentle squeeze when you feel ready." She held her breath and squeezed the trigger.

"Wow, great job," Linc said. "You hit the center mass on the target. Not bad for a newbie." He gave her a high five after she clicked the safety back on.

They spent a little more time talking about gun safety and how and where she should carry the pistol. Two hours later Brigid was finally starting to feel comfortable with it. After shooting numerous rounds and going through quite a few targets, she'd become fairly confident. As she was getting back into Linc's truck, she felt a lot better about the whole thing than she had when they'd arrived at the range.

"You did a great job. I'm impressed," Linc said as he started the truck.

"Thanks. I was kind of surprised myself," she said with a smile. Her cell phone began to ring, interrupting their conversation.

"Hello?" she answered, not recognizing the number on her cell phone screen.

"Hey, Brigid. This is Deputy Davis down at the sheriff's station. I was wonderin' if maybe ya' had a bit of time ya' could come down here? Sheriff Rich said you'd be willin' to help out with the case. I could sure use someone to brainstorm with fer a bit. He's gonna' be off fer a few days. It's all been a bit much for him. Can't say as I blame him."

"Sure. That's not a problem. I feel so bad for him. No one should have to see their sister like that. Poor man," she said. Linc was listening intently as he drove.

"Jes' wanted to make sure yer' on board. I wanna' get started soon as possible. Can't waste time in a case like this. Every minute counts, and Lucy deserves to have her killer brought to justice soon as possible."

"I completely agree, Deputy Davis. Give me about an hour, and I'll be there."

"Works for me. See ya' soon." The deputy hung up and Brigid put her phone away.

"What was that all about?" Linc asked.

"The deputy wants me to go down to the station and help him brainstorm on the case," she said as she looked out the window. "I hope I can help. Although I do pretty much know everyone around here, I'm still not entirely sure I can help."

Linc pulled into her driveway and shut off the truck. "Don't underestimate yourself, Brigid. Although you may not be well-versed in the law, that doesn't mean you can't help. If anything, you may be even more of an asset than someone who is. People might tell you things that they wouldn't tell an officer."

They got out of the truck and walked up to her door. "I hadn't thought of that, Linc, but you may be right." She remembered everything Missy had told her and wondered if she'd mentioned any of it to the deputies. Things were pretty much a blur after she and Missy discovered Lucy's body.

"Be careful and make sure you take Jett with you," Linc said.

"I will. I could use the company, so I'll be sure and take him with me. Thanks for being patient with me this morning." Linc went back to his truck and headed home while Brigid went inside her house to get Jett.

As soon as she got inside, her cell phone rang and she saw Missy's name on the screen. "Good morning Missy, how are you doing?" she asked as she answered the phone.

"I'm doing okay. How about you?" she asked.

"About the same. I'm getting ready to go down to the sheriff's office to talk to Deputy Davis. He wants me to help him with the case, since Sheriff Rich can't take it." Brigid opened the door to the back yard and stepped aside as Jett came trotting through the door.

"Tell him I'd be happy to help, too. I'm worried about Jordan. He's so upset. He feels like he let Lucy down," Missy said.

"Why does he feel that way?" Brigid asked as she headed towards the front door.

"I guess Lucy had wanted to meet with him, but he's been so busy lately he put it off for two days. He keeps thinking if he'd taken the time to talk to her, maybe she'd still be alive."

"Poor man. That's not his fault," Brigid said as she stood outside her house, waiting for Jett to take care of business before loading him in her car.

"I know, and on some level, he knows, too, but you know how that goes." Brigid could tell by Missy's sniffles that she was crying. "Oh, and Henri called our house late last night. He's devastated. He feels like the whole thing is his fault because he was so late getting home. He was a complete and total mess. He kept going on and on about how he didn't know if he could run the B & B all by himself."

"That doesn't surprise me. Lucy was excellent at staying on top of things. She really was a unique and strong woman." Brigid felt her throat tighten as she thought of her friend. "Missy, it's going to take time for all of us. It's not Henri's fault. At least I don't think it is. I mean, if any of us had known…," she let the thought trail off.

"I know. I told him I thought I knew someone at the church that could probably help him with the breakfast part of things. He said that was his main concern right now. He doesn't even know how to cook. He said they had people working for them who cleaned the rooms and did the yard maintenance. He's going to try to handle the check-ins and the registration stuff." Missy said.

"I'm sure he just needs time to figure things out. It can't be easy. Dealing with his emotions would be hard enough, and then to have to greet guests? I can't imagine," Brigid said with a sigh.

"I still can't believe she's gone, Brigid," Missy said tearfully.

"I know. It doesn't feel right. The whole world seems a bit darker without her in it."

CHAPTER FOURTEEN

"Good late morning, Corey. I hope you don't mind that I brought my dog, Jett, with me," Brigid said as she sat down across from the deputy at his desk. Deputy Davis looked much worse than he had the evening before. His eyes had dark circles under them and his complexion looked pale. Brigid wondered if he'd been up all night. He certainly looked like it. Papers littered his desk, and a half-eaten breakfast burrito sitting on a Styrofoam plate had been pushed to one side of his desk.

"Not at all. Maybe he can help, and I sure can use all the help I can get," he said with a smile as he looked at the big dog. "Talked to Rich this mornin'. Figgered we need to get started on a list of suspects like right now. He said Lucy was worried about some woman that got outta' prison a few months ago. I'm gonna' look into it and see if I can dig anythin' up. Maybe where she went when she left prison, or what she's been up to after bein' released."

"That seems like a good place to start," Brigid said. "Did he mention anything else?"

"He also talked about Henri. Said he never did like the guy, and he's suspected fer a long time he was havin' an affair with another woman. Said he'd never talked to Lucy about it, 'cuz he didn't wanna' hurt her. Rich felt that Henri was gone a whole lot more than takin' care of B & B business would justify.

"Tol' me he really wanted to go over there and confront him about everythin' this mornin' but thankfully I was here to talk him outta' it. Finally got him calmed down and convinced him to stay home. I tol' him I'd go talk to Henri 'bout it, but I gotta' tell ya', I ain't lookin' forward to it." Deputy Davis began to fidget with his pen.

"I can do that for you. Why don't you let me go over there?" Brigid asked. "As Lucy's friend, it would be much more natural for me to go over and ask him about it. I can't imagine anyone wanting to have that kind of conversation with a sheriff after their spouse was murdered. Especially if he didn't do it."

From what she knew about him, Brigid had always liked Henri. She couldn't believe he'd been having an affair and then murdered Lucy. That kind of betrayal would be the absolute worst.

"Ya' got a point," he said, thinking. "It'd only be natural for ya' to visit, kinda' like payin' yer' respects. Then ya' could maybe bring up you'd heard concerns 'bout their marriage." He picked up a pen and tapped it against his lips. "If he was cheatin' and then his wife goes and gets murdered, he's probably already feelin' purty guilty. No need to make him feel worse if he ain't our man."

When I said I'd help the deputy I had no idea anyone really butchered the English language like this. Next time I see Fiona I'll have to ask her about his background. I thought people only spoke like this in the books I edit.

"I agree," Brigid said. "I'll do that today. I can't make any promises, but I'll see what I can find out and get back with you. I'd feel better trying it this way first. If he is simply a grieving widower, I'd hate to be the one responsible for putting him through more pain. Did Rich mention anything else?"

"Only other person he could think of at the moment was the handyman for the B & B, Mike Loomis. Rich hates him. Said he woulda' busted him a while ago, but he worked for Lucy, and she said he was a good employee. Guess the guy has a bit of a record or somethin'. Mainly drug related, but from what Rich said, looks like he deals the hardcore stuff, and if he's dealin', dude's most likely usin'. Ya' know how them meth heads are capable of doin' anythin' when they're strung out on meth," he said with a sigh.

"Gotta' look into where he was at the time of the murder. Jes' might be a good suspect." Deputy Davis began to write in his notebook. "That's where I'm at right now. Got anythin' to add?" he asked.

"Maybe. Have you heard anything about a man named Ouray Smith?" she asked.

"Who is he?" he asked as he leaned forward, his pen ready.

"Apparently he's a somewhat local Native American man who was a guest at a book club meeting. He wrote a book on Chief Ouray, and the book club had it as their book of the month. He's big into preserving the heritage of the Ute tribe, and I understand Lucy mentioned to him she had some Ute artifacts. I heard he wasn't too fond of the idea, and I guess that would be putting it mildly. Anyway, he insisted she return them to the tribe. When she refused, he started harassing her."

"Ain't never heard of him," Corey said. "Better put him on the list. Don't hurt to check everyone out." He wrote the name down and dropped his pen.

"I agree, he might be a possible suspect. I'll see if I can find out more about him, too," Brigid said. "I guess I better get started. I'll head over to the B & B now and see what Henri has to say." Brigid picked up her purse and stood up, glad to be free of the hard-wooden chair she'd been sitting on.

"Lemme know what ya' find out. Don't leave nothin' out, ya' hear? I'll be waitin' fer yer' call."

"Absolutely. I'll get back to you as soon as I can," she said with a reassuring smile. She planned to tell him every little detail she came across. She was not going to let her best friend's killer get away.

"Come on Jett." She slapped her leg, and the dog quickly climbed to his feet. His nails clicked on the old tile floor as they headed for the door.

Jett stuck by Brigid's side as they approached her car. She opened the back door for him and said, "Climb on in, big guy," before shutting it behind him. Once in the driver's seat, Brigid dug her phone out of her purse and began to scroll through her contacts until she found her sister, Fiona. She pressed call and held the phone up to her ear.

"Fiona, it's Brigid. I've got a couple of quick questions for you," she said after her sister answered.

"What's up?" her sister asked from the other end.

"What can you tell me about Sheriff Rich's deputy, Corey Davis. He speaks the worst English I've ever heard. I'm an editor, and this is killing me."

Fiona laughed. "We've all thought the same thing, but the guy has a heart of gold. The only thing I know about him is that supposedly he was an orphan who was taken in by an old guy who didn't work, just hunted and fished. He raised Corey and from what I heard, when he was at the sheriff's academy he spoke perfect English. The guy is serious smart, but he talks like that because the guy who raised him talked like that. It's kind of a weird way to honor someone's memory, but kind of sweet at the same time."

"Thanks. Knowing that, I can handle it, it's just that my editor's brain spent the whole time I was with him inwardly correcting him. I'll have to let that go. Here's my second question. Remember that Ouray Smith guy you told me about?"

"Sure, what about him?" Fiona asked.

"I think since he'd been harassing Lucy, it would be worth it to pay him a little visit. Can you send me his address and anything else you might have about him?" Brigid asked.

"Sure. I have it all written down in my notebook. I'll take a picture of the page and send it to you, but why are you going to visit him? Isn't that the job of the sheriff department's?" Fiona asked.

"Probably, but it looks like I'm officially helping Deputy Davis. Here's what happened." She told Fiona about Rich's visit last night and her recent meeting with Deputy Davis. "Anyway, that's where I'm at. Thanks in advance for sending me the information about Ouray. I'll talk to you later," Brigid said, ending the call.

She'd started the car and was heading over to the B & B when she received a picture message from her sister with all of Ouray's contact information. "Perfect," she said out loud. Turning to Jett she said, "Now we know how to get ahold of him." Jett woofed as if he understood perfectly.

While she was saving the photo message to her phone, it began to ring. She saw that it was Linc and pressed the green answer icon. "Hi, Linc."

"Thought I'd check up on you and see how things are going," he said.

"They're going fine. Can I interest you in taking a ride later on today?" Brigid asked.

"Sure, where to?"

"Well, there's a guy I need to talk to, Ouray Smith. He's a Native American with the Ute tribe. The headquarters of the Ute Tribal Council is in Ignacio, but I just found out that Ouray lives only about an hour away from Cottonwood Springs. I thought I'd take a little drive over there and see what he knows."

"I'm assuming this is about Lucy's murder? Why do you need to talk to this guy?" Linc asked.

"Apparently he was pretty upset that Lucy had a large collection of Ute tribal artifacts she was using as decorations in the B & B, and he kept trying to convince her to hand them over to him. Of course, Lucy said no, but the guy got a bit forceful and was harassing her."

"I know who you're talking about. I stayed at the B & B for several days while I was waiting to move into my house, and one day they were having quite a heated discussion. I didn't stick around to see what it was all about. Didn't feel it was my business. Sure, I'll go with you."

"Great," Brigid said smiling. "I'll swing by and pick you up in about an hour." She ended the call, feeling good for the first time since she'd seen Lucy at the B & B. She knew she was doing everything she could to make sure her friend's killer was caught.

CHAPTER FIFTEEN

A short time later Brigid pulled into the B & B parking lot. Jett was sound asleep in the back seat. He was obviously dreaming, because his feet were twitching as if he was in hot pursuit of something, probably a squirrel or a chipmunk. Rather than trying to wake him, she rolled down the windows and quietly slipped out of the car. The gravel crunched under her tennis shoes as she approached the back door.

When she was at the kitchen door, she took a deep breath to calm herself and quietly knocked. This was completely new territory for Brigid. She had no idea how this was going to go, but she was fully committed to it. She had to talk to Henri. Even though Lucy was dead, Brigid felt some sort of explanation was needed from Henri as to what had been going on in their marriage.

Brigid knew she was probably going to have to ask some tough questions that were really none of her business, but she felt she had to for Lucy's sake. She saw Henri's big green extended cab truck parked in front of the garage, but there was no response to her knocks. After several minutes, she tried the doorknob. It turned and she quietly opened the door.

Peeking her head inside the kitchen, Brigid flashed back to when she saw Lucy lying dead on the floor. Her eyes couldn't help but linger on the spot as she stepped inside, quietly shutting the door.

She heard the gentle murmur of a voice and took a few steps closer to where it was coming from. She recognized Henri's voice speaking in rapid French.

One of Brigid's life-long dreams had been to go to France, and determined to do so, she'd been studying French in her spare time for the last two years. She'd come to a point where she could speak it and understand it, although she had to really concentrate to make out what Henri was saying, since he was speaking so fast.

"I'm going to have to tell the sheriff, Joelle," he was saying. "I know… but he is going to need to know where I was when Lucy was murdered. I don't like it any more than you do, but it must be done. They need to find out who killed Lucy, and as her husband, and because I wasn't there when she was murdered, I will probably be the number one suspect." He was quiet for some time and then continued, "I know my *cherié*, my sweet little butterfly. Don't worry. We will be together soon, but we have to wait a proper amount of time. To do it right away would make them look even closer at me."

Brigid remained very still, not wanting Henri to know she was listening to his phone conversation. Even if he did discover she'd overheard it, she was certain Henri would never suspect she'd understood what he had said because he was speaking French. She continued to listen, hoping to find out if he'd murdered Lucy or if he knew who had.

"Yes, it's a very good thing your cat got out last night. Otherwise, we wouldn't have anyone to vouch for us. Thankfully, your neighbor was outside, and can verify that we were nowhere near the B & B when Lucy was murdered. My brother-in-law, the sheriff, has never liked me much anyway, and he'll probably try to pin this on me."

There was a pause as Henri listened. "I hate to say this, *cherié*, but you will be a suspect, too." He listened for a moment and then said, "I understand, my sweet, but being the lover of the man who was married to the woman who was murdered in cold blood, does look a little bad, *n'est pas*? We need to keep our distance for a week or so. Just until everything calms down, and they catch the murderer. At least we both have an alibi. They cannot touch us. I love you, now I must go."

Brigid turned around and rapidly walked back towards the door when she heard him ending the call. She didn't want him to know she'd overheard his conversation. She hurried out the door and closed it, then turned and knocked loudly on it. This time, Henri answered the door.

"Oh, hello, Brigid," he said. "Please, come in."

"Thanks, Henri. I just want to tell you how sorry I am for your loss. Do you have a minute to talk to me, if that isn't too much trouble? Lucy was my best friend, and I know there were a few things bothering her lately. I thought you might be able to help me." Brigid didn't want to be too direct, but she knew if she wasn't direct, she didn't think Henri would answer honestly.

"Of course. I just made some tea. Would you like a cup?" Henri asked as he turned and began busying himself getting cups from the kitchen cabinet after Brigid nodded affirmatively. She pulled a chair out from the kitchen table and sat down.

"Thank you," she said as he handed her a warm cup of tea. She took a sip. She didn't know any other way to say it, so she decided to come out with it. "I really don't know how to say this Henri, so I might as well just say what I'm thinking. Lucy had suspected you were having an affair. Is it true?"

"Ah well, you see…" he began before pausing. "Yes, it's true. Our marriage wasn't the best. I will admit that. We'd drifted so far apart, I was certain there was no going back. It felt more like we were roommates, or that she was my boss rather than my wife. We barely even shared a bed. There was a woman in France I'd been seeing when I met Lucy, all those years ago. She found me on Facebook, and we started having conversations. One thing led to another.

"A year ago she came to the United States, and we reconnected," he said with a shrug. "You know how those things go. In France it is very common to have a mistress, but I don't think Lucy would have accepted such an arrangement. I'm not sure what would have happened to our marriage if Lucy hadn't been murdered. I didn't know what my future held while she was alive, and I don't know any more now that she is dead." He looked away from Brigid, as if he couldn't directly meet the eyes of Lucy's friend.

"Yes, I'm sure this is a confusing time for you," Brigid said softly. "What do you think you're going to do?" She couldn't imagine being in Henri's shoes. While she didn't approve of his actions, she really didn't think he'd meant for Lucy to get hurt, much less murdered.

"I think I may eventually return to France. Even after all these years, I still consider it my home. My heart is there. America is not where I want to spend the rest of my life. I will keep the B & B going for a while, for Lucy's sake. Beyond that, I doubt I will stick around." He held his hands up, looking around the kitchen. "Really, there is no reason for me to stay."

"I hate to ask you this, Henri, but where were you when Lucy was murdered?" Brigid already knew from the telephone call she'd overheard, but she wanted to see if he kept his story straight.

He looked embarrassed and said, "I was with my lover, Joelle. Her cat escaped out the door when we were coming back from dinner. We were out in front of her house looking for him when her neighbor arrived home. He helped us find the cat. It had made its way over into his yard and was sleeping in one of the flower pots on his patio. I made sure I wrote the neighbor's name and phone number down after what happened to Lucy. He can verify that we were both there."

"Good. I may need to talk to Joelle, though. You see, Deputy Davis has asked me to help him with the murder investigation, and I want to do it for Lucy," Brigid said. Joelle would probably say the same thing Henri had, but she felt that she'd be remiss if she didn't check it out. After all, wasn't that what the private investigators did in the murder mysteries she edited?

"Please don't, Brigid. I'd really prefer to keep our affair quiet. It would not reflect well on Lucy. She wouldn't have wanted people to know that sort of thing. I'll be happy to give you the information about the witness. Please, for Lucy's sake." Henri looked at her with pleading eyes.

Brigid was quiet for a moment as she debated whether she should talk to Joelle. She took another drink of tea to buy herself some time before she answered. "All right, Henri. I agree. Lucy would probably not want this made public. Let me have the information about the witness, so I can pass it along to the sheriff's deputy. Maybe we can keep Lucy's memory from being tainted by your actions," she said in a disapproving tone of voice. Brigid planned on telling Deputy Davis everything. If he felt Joelle needed to be interviewed, he would have to be the one to call her.

"Thank you. Here, let me give you the contact information I have for the neighbor." He took his phone out of his pocked and opened it. He wrote down the name, address, and phone number on a piece of paper and passed it across the table to Brigid. "I truly hope the killer is caught quickly. According to the deputy I talked to, Lucy didn't suffer for very long, and for that I'm grateful, if one can be grateful to a murderer. He said her death was relatively quick. She probably didn't even have time to understand what was happening to her."

"I sincerely hope so," Brigid said softly. "I'm still having trouble believing something like this could happen in Cottonwood Springs."

"I know, I'll be wondering about everyone I see until they find out who did it." Henri looked down into his cup, and Brigid noticed he looked exhausted. *Most likely he didn't sleep much last night, because he felt guilty for not being here when the killer attacked and smothered Lucy.* Brigid thought. *He was with his lover, how ironic.*

"I'll be going now. Thanks for the tea," Brigid said as she stood up and smiled at him. He stood up as well, looking like he might fall asleep on his feet. "Henri, let me give you a little advice. Try and get some sleep, you look like you could use it." She turned and started to walk out the door.

He nodded. "I think I will. All the guests are gone, and I have nothing else to do right now." Henri blamed himself for Lucy's murder. If he'd been home, she'd still be alive. He'd known that the affair he was having was wrong, but it never occurred to him anything would happen to Lucy while she was in the safety of their home. Even though he'd fallen out of love with her, that didn't mean he wanted to see her hurt. In his own way, he still cared for her, even if it wasn't outwardly evident.

Brigid stepped into the afternoon sunlight, but she still felt chilled. Henri and his lover were off the short list of suspects, which was a good thing. Although it meant her friend hadn't been murdered by her unfaithful husband or his lover, it still meant the murderer was at large in the community of Cottonwood Springs.

The thought that it could be anyone struck Brigid as she got back in her car. Driving down the road, she paid special attention to everyone she saw, people out walking, people driving in their cars, everyone. Was Lucy's killer someone she'd grown up with? Or maybe it had been someone passing through Cottonwood Springs. Brigid couldn't understand what the motive might have been. She couldn't think of any situation where killing someone would seem like the only option, and especially someone like Lucy who was always ready to help anyone who needed it. Who would want to murder someone like Lucy?

CHAPTER SIXTEEN

As she was driving away from the B & B, Brigid felt conflicted. On one hand she was glad her friend hadn't been murdered by her husband or his lover. That would have been entirely too heartbreaking. But on the other hand, knowing that her friend's husband had been having an affair that would have hurt her friend deeply didn't make her feel very good. Now that she could pretty much cross Henri and Joelle off the suspect list, it was time to visit another possible suspect.

Jett woke up just as they were pulling into Linc's driveway. When Linc stepped out of the front door, Jett began to get excited, jumping and barking in the back seat. The dog was so big, the car rocked with the weight of his body moving around.

"Jett, calm down," Brigid said with a laugh as she climbed out of the car and opened the back door for Jett. He launched himself, whining and barking, off the seat and rushed towards Linc, who had to be careful not to get bowled over by the big, excited dog.

"Hey, boy, I'm happy to see you too," he said as he greeted the dog, making sure his feet were firmly planted. He looked over at Brigid. "How did everything go?" he asked as he tried to calm Jett down.

"Not too bad," she said, watching the two play for a moment

before they turned towards her car. "I think we can safely mark two possible suspects off the list."

Linc opened the back door for Jett, and then he got in the front seat. "Who's that?" he asked after Brigid got behind the wheel and they were in the process of fastening their seatbelts.

As she started the car, she said, "Henri and his girlfriend. Apparently, he's been having an affair with some woman named Joelle that he knew from years ago when he lived in France. Both of them have a solid alibi. They were returning to her home after dinner when her cat ran out the front door. While they were searching for it, a neighbor pulled up and helped them find the cat. Henri told me the neighbor can verify they were there at the time Lucy was murdered. What do you think?"

"I think it's a pretty good sign they aren't the killers, but it doesn't make him look very good. What he was doing is pretty sleazy. Nobody likes a cheat, particularly a man who was cheating on his wife at the very time she was murdered." Linc sighed. "That's really sad. So where did you tell me we are headed out to and why?"

Brigid looked over at him and smiled. "We're going to see Ouray Smith. He's the Native American guy you told me you saw at the B & B when you were staying there. We're going to try and find out where he was when Lucy was murdered."

"Brigid, let me ask you something," Linc said as he turned in his seat to face her. "You've had a little time to think about it now. Who do you think did it?"

"I'm not really sure," Brigid mused. "I probably would have thought it was Henri or Joelle. That would make the most sense. Either one of them could have felt that the only way for them to be together was for something bad to happen to Lucy. Besides, isn't that usually the case?" Brigid paused, thinking of the books she'd edited. It was often the spouse or a lover who committed the crime.

"Deputy Davis said the handyman at the B & B was a suspect, but that doesn't feel right to me. Just because he's into drugs doesn't necessarily make him a killer, and since he was working for Lucy, why would he want to kill her?"

Linc thought about it for a moment, "Maybe she threatened to turn him in or fire him?" He shrugged his shoulders. "What kind of drugs does he supposedly do?"

"I guess he sells meth and most likely does it, too." Brigid leaned on the door as she thought more about the possibility of him being a suspect.

"Well if it's true that he's doing meth, you never know what he could be capable of. From what I understand, some people on that stuff go days without sleeping. They almost lose their minds. If he was strung out, and she said the wrong thing one time…" Linc let his sentence trail off.

"I suppose that's true. I just don't know much about drugs," she said.

"I watch a lot of true crime shows," Linc said as he looked at the passing scenery. "The way people mess up their lives just fascinates me." They lapsed into silence for a few minutes before he started talking again. "Anyone else on your list of possible suspects?"

"Let's see," Brigid said as she thought about the possible suspects. "We have the husband, his lover, the handyman, Ouray, who we're going to check out now…" she paused for a moment. "Oh yeah, and a woman that Lucy testified against in a criminal case years ago."

"Lucy testified against someone?" Linc asked. "What was that all about?"

"The way I understand it," Brigid began, "is this woman was embezzling money from the ski resort. Fiona's husband, Brandon, who is the manager of the ski resort, asked Lucy if she could help them figure out what was up with their books. They'd found some discrepancies, and she was always really good with figures. Once she went through them, Lucy figured out where the money was going and told her brother, the sheriff. The woman was arrested for embezzlement, found guilty, and sent to prison."

"Whoa," Linc said, "but if she's in prison, how could she be the killer?"

"Here's the thing. A couple of years ago, Lucy had a couple who were staying at her B & B, and they became good friends. The husband happened to be a guard at the prison where this woman was serving her prison term. They had a conversation one night about crimes that had happened in Cottonwood Springs. It's a small world. The guard knew the woman Lucy had testified against. Lucy had been worried she might try to get even with her when she got out of prison, and the guard said he'd let her know if she was released on parole. He called not too long ago and told Lucy that the woman had been released from prison."

"I can understand why Lucy was worried. I would have been too," Linc said.

"I sure would think so, and it seems with good reason." Brigid rolled her shoulders, feeling the tension there. "That's the list of possible suspects for now, Linc. I really don't see Ouray as being the murderer, but he still needs to be checked out."

"I agree." said Linc. "Some ancient Native American artifacts don't seem like a reason to commit murder, but just read the papers or listen to the news. People have sure killed over less."

A little later they pulled up outside a tiny unkempt house that looked as if it was abandoned. White paint had long since faded and begun to chip. One window was boarded up while another had the shutter dangling from it at an odd angle. The yard was overgrown with weeds and large dead rose bushes lined the front of the house. Brigid double-checked the address to make sure they were at the right place.

She put the car in park and leaned back. "According to the

address Fiona gave me, this should be the place." Brigid leaned over and they both looked out the passenger side window, neither one of them too anxious to walk up to the house. It was depressing to look at, and there was nothing welcoming about it.

"Well, as long as we're here, we might as well see if he's home," Linc said. When they were out of the car, Linc looked back at Jett and said, "Think Jett better get out too. At the very least, he can stretch his legs. Hopefully, he'll get the hint that we'd like him to commune with nature, too."

When Jett was finished, the three of them walked up the uneven walkway to the front door. Weeds were growing through the cracks, and Brigid and Linc had to be careful not to trip. The closer they got to the house, the worse it looked. The windows were so dirty Brigid doubted that any light could get in. The other houses along the street were just as small but looked well taken care of. The lawns were freshly mowed and children were playing outside.

While Linc was knocking on the door an older brown sedan pulled into the driveway next door. A man got out of the car and said in a loud voice, "He's not home." He began to take grocery bags from the back seat.

"Excuse me?" Brigid said. She stepped away from the house and took a few steps towards where the man was standing.

"You lookin' for Ouray?" the man asked. When Brigid nodded, he continued, "He's not home. Left early this mornin' for a tribal meetin' in Ignacio. He goes every month, although he almost didn't go today. He was pretty worried about it last night."

"Why's that?" Linc asked as he joined Brigid.

The man set his bags on the trunk of his car and walked to the side of his driveway. "Well, his truck's been givin' him trouble lately. Just not runnin' right. He's no mechanic, I can tell you that, so I came over to help him out a bit. Took a while, but we finally got it runnin' right. He just needed to re-set his lifters. Took most of the night, but she was purring like a kitten by the time we were done." The man smiled and crossed his arms, obviously proud of the work he'd done.

"So he was here last night?" Brigid asked. She and Linc walked back down the walkway and up the man's driveway, not wanting to walk through the dead grass and weeds in Ouray's front yard. Jett followed them, staying close to Brigid.

"Sure was. I got home about 4:00 yesterday afternoon, and I saw him messin' with his truck in the driveway. I could tell he was having problems, 'cuz he was cussing a blue streak." The man chuckled. "He told me what the truck was doin', so I went in and changed my clothes before I started helpin' him. We worked on that old truck until about 10:00 last night. I know it was that late because when I finally got inside, the 10 o'clock news was just comin' on the TV. Watch it every night."

"What's Ouray like?" Brigid asked. She was trying to get a picture of the man who had been harassing her friend. Was he just temperamental or was he capable of murder?

"Guy's intense, I'll tell you that. He's a member of the Ute tribe and says he's a descendant of Chief Ouray himself. I guess that's who he's named after. Anyway, he's got a real hot button for folks who collect Native American artifacts, more specifically Ute artifacts. Thinks every Native American item is sacred and should be returned to its tribe." The man sighed, "Well I better get goin'. Wish I could talk more, but today's my day off and I promised my wife I'd cook supper. Been a pleasure talkin' to you," he said as he picked up the grocery bags. "Want me to give Ouray a message?"

Linc looked over at Brigid, but she shook her head, "No, thanks. I think you answered our questions. Good luck with supper." She smiled at the man. He began to whistle as he headed toward his front door, and the three of them walked back to Brigid's car.

CHAPTER SEVENTEEN

"It looks like Ouray has an alibi, don't you agree?" Linc asked as Brigid pulled away from the rundown house that he called home.

"Sure seems to. If he was here working on a broken-down truck until 10:00 last night, there's no way he could have been in Cottonwood Springs to murder Lucy. It's pretty cut and dried. So he's another person who can be crossed off the suspect list," Brigid sighed. "My suspect list is getting short fairly quickly."

"Isn't that a good thing?" Linc asked.

"I suppose so. I'm beginning to think that I'm not cut out for this sort of thing. I'm sure not having much luck so far."

"What do you mean?" Linc asked, with a concerned look on his face.

"This investigating stuff. I feel like maybe I should just stick to editing. I'm just spinning my wheels, getting nowhere. It seems that all I'm doing is crossing people off the suspect list, and I'm sure not any closer to figuring out who did it."

Linc laughed. "Bet Sherlock Holmes and Miss Marple felt the same way at times. I don't think you're doing too bad. I'm sure Deputy Davis will appreciate what you've found out. You've saved him a lot of time." He noticed Brigid wasn't smiling. "Brigid, you're doing a fine job." He put his hand on her shoulder. "Who knows what Deputy Davis has come up with, and the fact that you've been able to cross three people off of a list of suspects is no simple feat."

"You really think so?" she asked as she turned to briefly look at him before she looked back at the road ahead of her.

"Absolutely. You've definitely been a big help today. Sometimes these things take time, lots of time. Lucy's killer is going to be caught. You believe that, don't you?"

"I think so. No, I believe it. If it's someone local, there's no way they'll get away with it. You're right, I just need to give it time." She smiled. "I do have an odd feeling about this prison lady, though."

"Oh? Why's that?" Linc asked as he settled back into his seat.

"If she was here before, that means she's somewhat local. Don't you think someone would notice if a woman who was once arrested for embezzlement at the ski resort came back to town?" Brigid shrugged. "You'd think word would get around pretty quickly. I mean, this is a small town, and everybody pretty much makes it a point to know everyone else's business."

"I get what you're saying, and I agree. Maybe Deputy Davis will have some more information about her when you talk to him and tell him what you've found out today."

They headed back to Cottonwood Springs with Jett sitting in the back seat, calmly watching the scenery go by. "I told Deputy Davis I'd stop by the station when I was finished to tell him what I'd found out. Want to ride along or do you need to head back home?" Brigid asked as they entered town.

"Sure. I don't have anything better to do. I'll go along for the ride," Linc said with a smile.

While Brigid was navigating the streets toward the sheriff's office, she thought, *there aren't many more suspects and unfortunately the ones I've marked off seemed to be the most plausible. I hope I'm not missing something.*

Her biggest fear was that Lucy was murdered by some random person just passing through, and they would have no way to track the person down. They could just roam free, hurting anyone they pleased, or worse. She couldn't let the search for the killer end like that.

Brigid was seemingly lost in thought when she parked her car outside the sheriff's office. "Hey," Linc said, touching her arm and interrupting her thoughts. "You sure you're okay?" He could tell she badly wanted to solve the case, but was frustrated by the lack of progress. He just hoped she didn't get hurt in the process.

"Yeah, sorry. I'm just worried we won't be able to figure out who the killer is. I can't stand the thought of having my friend's murderer getting off scot free." She took a long steadying breath.

"Don't worry, Brigid," Linc said as he took her hand and gently squeezed it. "I have faith whoever did it won't get away with it."

"Thanks. Wish I felt the same way. I'm so glad Deputy Davis is on the case. He seems like he's really good at his job, and I'm glad he could cover for Rich. There is no way Rich could have handled this on his own. Poor guy. I can't imagine what he's going through. Being a law enforcement officer and having your sister murdered in your jurisdiction has to be your worst nightmare. That's about as bad as it gets." She hesitated for a moment, deep in thought and then said, "Linc, you don't think that might have had something to do with the murder, do you?"

"What do you mean?" Linc asked. "Rich being the sheriff?"

"Yes. What if someone wanted to punish Rich because he'd arrested them or something? What if rather than hurting him, they decided to hurt Lucy?" The more Brigid thought about it, the more concerned she became. "I don't know how many people would be on that kind of a list, but I'd bet it's a lot. Linc, there's no way we could find all of them. It would be like looking for a needle in a haystack. Think about it. Rich must have arrested hundreds of people during the years he's been in law enforcement. Any one of them could have a grudge against Rich and want to get even with him by killing Lucy."

"Hate to say it, but you could be right. I wouldn't worry about that possibility yet. We haven't even eliminated all the suspects on your list. Let's take care of that first, but I agree, it's something to consider if we take the remaining two off the list. Come on, let's go check in with the deputy," Linc said as he opened his car door.

Linc, Brigid and Jett entered the sheriff's office just as two deputies brought in a disheveled-looking man in handcuffs. His hair looked like it hadn't been washed in days. His jeans had grass stains and mud on them, almost as if he'd been tackled and thrown on the ground.

The sheriff's office had windows along the front of the building with an old wooden counter separating the back of the office, where a handful of desks were located, from the front of the office. A row of hard plastic chairs was located in the front office area. A hallway on the right side of the building led to the holding cells at the back of the building. The door to Rich's office was closed, and the light was off. Just seeing his door closed triggered memories of finding Lucy and made Brigid's chest constrict.

With a furious tone in his voice, Deputy Davis said to the dirty looking man, "What we got here?" He turned to Linc and Brigid. "Sorry, Brigid. Gimme' jes' a minute." He looked sternly at the man in handcuffs. "Rich gave ya' a second chance but ya' seemed to think it was a smart idea to start sellin' drugs to ski lodge guests anyway. Know what? Yer' disgustin'. That's what. Good thing one of the guests called us. Suppose the only positive side to all this is that I can't arrest ya' for Lucy's murder, not that I wouldn't like to, but ya' just happened to be tryin' to sell them drugs at the same time she was murdered. Witnesses and everythin' confirms that."

"Guess this is your luckiest bad day. 'Specially since Sheriff Jennings ain't here today. Don't think I coulda' restrained him. Them handcuffs woulda' been the least of your worries. Rich let ya' off last time 'cuz you'd been such a big help to his sister, but that was then and this is now. Hope ya' like the color green, since you're gonna' be wearin' jail house green fer quite a while." Deputy Davis turned to the two officers and said disgustedly, "Take him back to one of the holding cells." They escorted the man towards the hallway and disappeared.

"Sorry 'bout that," Deputy Davis said a bit more calmly to Brigid and Linc. He walked to the wooden counter and opened the half door indicating for them to enter.

"Not a problem," said Brigid. "Corey, this is Linc Olson. He lives next door to me, and he's been helping me out today."

Both men shook hands. "Thanks, Linc. I feel better about her helpin' me now that I know she's got someone watchin' her back."

"I am, but don't forget about Jett. Think he's watching her back, too." He reached down and petted the big dog who was standing next to Brigid.

"Well, looks like I jes' marked 'nother possible suspect off the list. That was Mike Loomis who jes' got escorted back to the holding cell. He's the handyman fer Lucy's B & B, or should I say he was the handyman fer the B & B. He was tryin' to make a drug deal out at the ski lodge at the time of the murder. Not real bright thing fer him to do, but it takes him off the suspect list. Too bad. I woulda' loved to arrest him fer murder, but we got a witness who can verify he was at the ski lodge at the time of the murder. No way he coulda' done it." he sighed. "He was clear out on the other side of town. Now, tell me ya' got some good news fer me."

They followed him to his desk and sat down. "Well, depends how you look at it." Brigid said. "We went to visit Henri. Turns out he was with his lover, Joelle, a woman he's been having an affair with. They have a witness, a neighbor, who will confirm they were at Joelle's house at the time of the murder. I guess Joelle's cat got out and the neighbor helped find it. Neither Henri nor his lady friend was anywhere near the B & B when Lucy was murdered. I have the witness' contact info if you want it."

"Good job," Deputy Davis said as he took notes. "Anythin' else?" He looked up from his yellow notepad.

"We drove over to visit Ouray Smith, the Native American guy who'd been harassing Lucy. Turns out his truck was broken down last night. We talked to a neighbor who said he'd helped Ouray fix it. He said they worked on it most of the afternoon yesterday and didn't finish up until about 10:00 last night."

"Looks like we can cross him off the list as well." Deputy Davis said as he leaned back in his chair. "That's about it fer our suspects, 'cept fer the mystery woman who Lucy testified against in that embezzlement case. I got a few feelers out fer her. Hope to know more in the mornin'." He put his feet up on his desk.

"Do you think that woman did it?" asked Brigid. "Do you think there really is a possibility she showed up in town and nobody noticed her?"

"I get what yer' saying. Ya' jes' never know. I wasn't with the sheriff's department then, so I don't know nuthin' 'bout that case. Always a possibility the woman was originally from a neighborin' town. Folks around here might not recognize her, 'specially if she's gained weight or changed somethin' 'bout her appearance," he said with a shrug. "But I'd imagine if someone who was caught for embezzlin' showed back up, word'd get around."

"That's what I was thinking," Brigid said. "Corey, if this woman gets crossed off the list, we're out of suspects."

"Where are you goin' with this, Brigid?" He was glad Rich had asked her to help. She'd already saved him a whole day of leg work.

"Well, I got to thinking, if this woman doesn't pan out, we're going to have to start a whole new list. What if Lucy was murdered because she was the sister of the sheriff and someone wanted to get back at him by killing her?"

Corey turned and looked at his boss' closed door before looking back at Brigid. "That'd be a very long list of possible suspects."

"My thoughts exactly," sighed Brigid. She leaned over and absentmindedly ran her hand down Jett's black furry back.

"Let's hope it don't come to that. We'll worry 'bout that after I get some info back on the mystery woman. Guess all we can do now is jes' wait. You were a big help today, Brigid. You too, Linc. Why don't ya' both go home and try to relax. I'm sure this has been taxin' on you, as well."

"Definitely," Brigid said, "but I'm glad to help."

"Thank you." Corey took his feet off of his desk and stood up as Brigid and Linc did the same. "I'll call soon as I know somethin'." He turned to Linc and said, "Nice meetin' ya." They shook hands again. "Linc, do me a favor and keep an eye on Brigid 'til this whole thing's over. If our murderer finds out she's helpin'…" He let his sentence trail off.

"You got it." said Linc. "I've been thinking the same thing. Between Jett and me, she'll be fine."

"Glad we're on the same page," Corey said as he followed them to the wooden counter. He bent down and scratched Jett's ear.

Linc and Brigid were both quiet as they walked back to her car.

CHAPTER EIGHTEEN

"Well, at least he seems to think I've done something that's helped. That makes me feel better," Brigid said as she pulled away from the sheriff's station.

"You did a good job today. Actually, you did a great job."

"Thanks, Linc," Brigid said. "I'm just trying to do what's right for Lucy."

"You're a very special person, Brigid. Not only have you dropped everything in your life to help find your friend's murderer, but you're not even worried about your own personal safety."

"Thanks for the compliment, but I'm not feeling all that special now. I just want to find Lucy's murderer."

Linc looked over at her and smiled. "I understand, but I still think you're special." As he was looking over at her and realizing how much he respected Brigid, she yawned.

"I have an idea," Linc said as Brigid drove toward their street. "You've got to be exhausted from everything today. Let me cook dinner for you. I'm actually a fairly good cook, and if I do say so myself, I'm great at making Italian food. I'll cook you my specialty, fresh pasta with a basil pesto sauce."

Brigid yawned again. "Thanks, Linc, but you really don't need to go to the trouble. I can make a sandwich or something." She really appreciated how helpful Linc had been, and it wasn't that she didn't want to spend more time with him, she actually wanted the opposite. She didn't want him to feel obligated or something just because they'd spent the day together.

"No, I insist." Linc said in a firm voice.

"That does sound inviting," she said as she pulled up outside his house. "I'll take Jett home and feed him, and I probably should check on my house guest, too. You know, make sure she's okay. I'll be back in about an hour if that's all right with you."

"Perfect," Linc said as he got out of the car. "See you in an hour."

Brigid drove the short distance down the street to her house and pulled into the driveway. "You ready to eat, Jett?" she asked. "You've had a pretty exciting day, too, haven't you?" She opened the car door for him, and they walked into the house.

After pouring a bowl of kibble into Jett's dog dish and refilling his water bowl, Brigid headed down the hall toward her room. She felt like she needed to change clothes and freshen up a bit. As she was walking down the hall, she passed by the guest bedroom. The door was open, and she looked in the room to see if Rachele was sitting at the desk with her laptop like she normally was. Instead, the chair was empty, and Brigid could easily see the screen on her laptop. There was a news article about Lucy's death displayed on it.

That's odd, Brigid thought. *Why would Rachele be interested in the murder of someone she didn't even know? Well I suppose she was just curious about it, particularly since Rich was here last night.*

While she was considering it, Brigid heard the toilet flush and the bathroom door opened. "Hi, Brigid," Rachele said. "I'm glad you're home. I want to show you something." She walked down the hall to the guest room, headed for her laptop, and then proceeded to open a Word document. "Thanks to you, my writer's block is gone. I am officially unblocked, and I've been writing up a storm."

"That's great," Brigid said as she stepped into the room and looked at the monitor. "I'm so happy for you."

"I couldn't have done it without you. Being here in Cottonwood Springs, even for this short amount of time, has made all the difference in the world to me. I bought a plane ticket for tomorrow, so I can head back home to Los Angeles, and I'm taking my writing muse with me." She grinned and ran her fingers through her hair.

"I'm glad I could help," Brigid said as she hugged Rachele. "Jett and I have plans to eat dinner with Linc. Do you need anything before we go?"

"No, but thanks. You and Jett have fun with Linc."

"What time does your flight leave tomorrow?" Brigid asked.

"The flight's at 4:00 in the afternoon, but I'll be leaving from here around noon since the airport's a couple of hours away and I need to return my rental car," she said with a sigh. "It feels good to be writing again."

"I'm sure it does. I'll see you later, Rachele. Linc's waiting for us, and I still need to change clothes and freshen up."

Brigid walked down the hall to her bedroom and shut the door behind her. She opened her closet door and pulled out a little nicer outfit than she'd been wearing earlier in the day. Even so, it was still casual. She was not in the mood to wear something constrictive or have her toes pinched trying to wear trendy shoes.

As she was taking off her clothes, Brigid couldn't help but think about what she'd seen in Rachele's room. Something about her having the article about Lucy's death up on her computer screen didn't feel right. Brigid could understand if she'd been reading it in passing, but supposedly she'd been writing her book. Why wouldn't that be on her monitor instead?

Brigid stepped into her bathroom, quickly washed her face, and began to reapply her makeup. She supposed Rachele could have just run across the article when she was researching something. Brigid knew that was something she did all the time. There was always that possibility, but something about it bothered her. Why would a woman who had never been to Cottonwood Springs be interested in a small-town murder? No matter how she turned it around in her mind, it didn't make sense to her.

She decided to talk to Linc about it and see what he thought. Looking at herself one more time in the mirror, she stepped out of her room and headed down the hall. She stopped at Rachele's door and saw that she was busily typing. "Rachele, as far as I know, I don't have any plans tomorrow morning. How about if I make you a celebration 'The Muse Has Returned' breakfast before you leave?"

Rachele turned away from her computer and smiled. "That sounds great, Brigid. Thanks. Have a good time with Linc tonight. I'll probably be in bed by the time you get home, so I'll see you in the morning."

"Okay, see you then." Brigid turned away from the door and continued down the hall. *It's been a long day,* she thought. *Maybe I'm just reading too much into things. I'm sure she has a perfectly reasonable explanation for the article being on her computer screen. I'll ask her in the morning.* "Come on, Jett. Time to go to Linc's."

Jett had climbed up on his loveseat, but once he heard Linc's name he jumped down on the floor, tail wagging. Brigid picked up her purse and stepped outside. For a moment she thought about walking to Linc's house, but decided against it. She had no idea how long she'd be at his house, and the last thing she wanted to do was walk on a dark road while there was a killer loose. She loaded Jett into the back seat of her car and backed down her driveway.

Linc greeted them at the door, and when they walked through it, she was greeted with a broad array of wonderful aromas. It was the first time she'd been in his home. It was a blend of modern architecture and rustic country. The metal beams went beautifully with the rough wood planks. It was industrial and open, masculine and rustic.

The lighting was muted, and she spent some time looking at the books in the wall of bookshelves located at the far end of the living room. A large flat screen television hung over the fireplace with an oversized dark blue couch and chair nearby.

Linc showed her the living room before he led Brigid to the large kitchen and poured her a glass of wine. Like the living room, the kitchen had an industrial look that went well with the country style. The cabinets were a warm oak with a beautiful grain. There was an island in the center with a sink, topped with black granite counter tops, which surprisingly, went well with the oak.

"Everything's ready for dinner but the pasta, so we have a few minutes to sit and unwind." He pulled a chair out from the round oak table tucked in the corner and offered it to Brigid. Once she was seated he hurried back to the stove. "My grandmother, my mother's mother, was full Italian. She always said, 'Pasta waits for no man,' and I've taken that to heart. Plus, I've found it to be fairly accurate. You have to pay attention to it, and stop cooking it at just the right moment or else it's not very good." He turned around and looked at Brigid. "Hey, are you alright? You seem kind of quiet. Is something wrong?"

Brigid shook her head and took a large swallow of wine. "I don't know, Linc, yes, I have an uneasy feeling that something's not right." She paused and studied the wood grain on Linc's cabinets. He dropped the pasta in the boiling water and returned to the table. When he was seated he gave her his full attention.

"When I went home to feed Jett, I walked down the hall to my bedroom to change clothes. On the way I passed by the guest room where Rachele's staying, and I glanced in her room. She was in the bathroom at the time, but on her computer screen there was an article about Lucy's murder. Something about that just didn't seem right, you know? It seems strange to me. I mean, she didn't even know Lucy, so why would she want to read an article about her murder?" Brigid's brow was furrowed in frustration.

Linc thought for a moment before answering. "I really have no idea, but I agree, that does seem a bit odd." He stood and walked over to the stove and looked at the pot of lightly boiling pasta, stirring it gently as he thought about the situation. "Brigid, what do you know about Rachele? It hadn't crossed my mind before now, but didn't she show up right before Lucy was murdered?"

Brigid's eyes became wide as she realized what Linc had just said. "You don't think she murdered Lucy, do you?" She felt like ice water was running down the middle of her back and she shivered involuntarily. When she heard him say it out loud, she felt her insides quiver. As they looked at each other, digesting the enormity of what he'd just said, Brigid's cell phone began to ring.

CHAPTER NINETEEN

Brigid kept her eyes on Linc's as she took her phone out of her purse and answered it.

"Brigid, I'm sorry to bother you. This is Deputy Davis. I jes' had a disturbin' phone call, and I really feel ya' should know about it," Corey said.

"No problem, Corey. What's wrong?" Linc began to drain the pasta into a colander as he listened to Brigid's side of the conversation.

"Well, I think I mighta' tol' ya' this, but I'll tell you again. I 'membered several months ago Rich mentionin' somethin' 'bout some guests Lucy had. Said she really liked 'em. The couple stayed at the B &B fer a week and durin' that time they became fast friends with Lucy. The husband worked fer the Colorado State Prison Authority.

"One time durin' breakfast Lucy told him about a woman who'd been convicted fer embezzlin' money from the local ski resort based on testimony Lucy gave against her during her trial. The guard actually knew the woman. When she was paroled from prison, he called Lucy to give her a head's up. Rich said it really scared her, knowin' the woman was free. Up 'til now, that was all I'd heard."

"And now what have you heard?" Brigid asked anxiously.

"I jes' got off the phone with that prison guard. He saw an article 'bout Lucy's murder and was really shaken up by it. Said he and his wife really liked Lucy, so he wanted to know if it was the woman who was paroled that had done it. Tol' him I had no information on her yet and that we hadn't had any strangers in town, leastways not to my knowledge, so I doubted it."

"Corey, wait," Brigid interrupted. "That's not true. For work I edit books. One of my authors came to stay with me because she was having problems with what we call writer's block. I told her if she got out of Los Angeles she might find herself a bit more inspired. She came here to Cottonwood Springs the day before yesterday." Brigid's heart felt like it might burst out of her chest. She felt goosebumps on the back of her neck.

"Yer' tellin' me she showed up the day before Lucy was murdered?" Corey asked incredulously. "Little too coincidental fer my taste, Brigid."

Brigid's eyes met Linc's. She knew he was thinking the same thing. "Mine too," she answered softly.

"Bob, that's the guard's name, told me what he could 'bout the woman. She started writin' when she was in prison and seemed to be purty good at it. She tol' him she wrote fiction. She even had an editor in Los Angeles and was making good money. Said there was all kinds of books and writing material in her cell."

Brigid's blood had run cold. She was an editor from Los Angeles. "Corey, by any chance did he tell you her name?"

Linc was fully concentrating on the conversation. He'd moved closer to Brigid, so he could hear both sides. He feared the same thing Brigid did.

"Yeah, I wrote it down. Let me see, ah, here it is. Name's Rachele Peters."

Linc got Brigid's attention and slid his finger across his throat. "Hang up," he mouthed.

CHAPTER TWENTY

"Now what?" Brigid asked Linc with a worried look on her face. "That's the woman who's staying in my home." She felt panicked at the thought she may have been housing a murderer but at the same time, she was angry. How dare this woman take advantage of her hospitality. What kind of a person would do something like that?

Another part of her felt somewhat responsible for Lucy's death, and it was not a good feeling. If she hadn't invited Rachele to come to Cottonwood Springs to get rid of her writer's block, Lucy might still be alive. She felt sick to her stomach. She'd had a feeling when she'd agreed to let Rachele stay with her that she'd regret her decision. She knew now she'd regret it the rest of her life.

"Now we know why you saw the article about Lucy on her computer screen," Linc said as he paced back and forth across the tile kitchen floor, the pasta forgotten. He stopped and looked at Brigid. "She was keeping an eye on the story, trying to see if the sheriff had any leads. Your hunch was absolutely right about something being off about the whole thing. Give me the gun I gave you this morning. We need to get over to your house right now and make sure she doesn't get away."

He turned and looked at Jett. "I want you to keep Jett right by your side. If there's a problem just tell him 'attack'. Most dogs that are well trained are taught that command. Let's just hope whoever trained him did the same. We don't have time to wait for Deputy Davis to get here. Let's get going."

He took the gun Brigid handed him and said, "We can't take the car because she'd hear us. We'll walk towards your house and stay hidden in the trees behind our houses. That way, we can sneak over to your house without being seen. Come on." He gestured for her to follow him as he headed toward the back door. Brigid whistled for Jett, and he followed close behind her.

The sun was starting to fade behind the distant clouds as they hurried to the treeline behind the houses. The cedars were particularly fragrant as they crunched through the underbrush. Jett stayed close to Brigid, sensing the tension in the air. Linc was in the lead, the gun in his hand, ready to fire if needed.

This is insane, Brigid thought. *I can't believe I'm sneaking over to my own house in hopes of catching a killer. And not only that, I'm the one who invited her to come and stay with me.* She took a deep breath as she navigated through the brush, staying as close to Linc as possible. *So much for trying to be nice. How was I supposed to know she was from here and held some kind of a grudge against Lucy? She never mentioned anything about it. This whole writer's block thing was probably just a way to get here, and I took the bait, hook, line, and sinker.*

A few minutes later, they were directly behind Brigid's house. They paused for a minute or two while they watched the house. Linc and Brigid ducked down behind a large bush, silently hoping it was dark enough and they were far enough away that Rachele wouldn't see them if she happened to look out the window. The lights in a couple of rooms were on, one of which was Rachele's room. They watched as she moved back and forth across the room.

"Looks like she's packing," Brigid whispered. "I bet she's planning to leave early. She probably thought my having dinner at your house was the perfect time to leave. She'd leave the door closed to her room, so when I got home I'd think she was asleep, which would give her plenty of time to get away from Cottonwood Springs. I even let her put her car in my garage. Clever woman."

"Definitely possible," Linc said as they continued to watch. When Rachele had finished walking back and forth from the closet to the bed, Linc turned to Brigid. "I want to go around to the front of the house. If we go in the back and she slips out the front door, she'll be able to get in her car. We'd have no way to chase her, because both of our cars are at my house. She'd be out of here in a matter of seconds.

"Here's my plan. Follow me around the side of the house and stay right behind me. We'll sneak around and come in through the front. All we need to do is corner her. She won't be able to leave the house." He waited for Brigid to nod before they jogged softly up to the house. They slipped along the side of the house, concealed by the chest-high bushes growing along that side of the house. Jett stayed right on Brigid's heels, never more than half a step away from her. She was pretty impressed at what Jett was instinctively doing. She'd never trained him to act as a guard dog. It was as if he knew exactly what was required of him.

As she crept along the side of her home, Brigid felt her hands begin to shake. She wasn't sure if it was caused by nerves or the rage that was building inside her. It had started out small, but the closer they got to the front of the house, the stronger the sensation became. She felt she'd been used and her trust violated. It was not a good feeling.

Linc knelt down at the corner of the house that led to the front. He turned and held up one finger to his lips signaling to Brigid that she should remain quiet, before carefully peeking around the corner. Jett nudged Brigid affectionately. She smiled and scratched behind his ears. Once Linc was sure Rachele wasn't in the front yard, he signaled for Brigid and Jett to follow him.

They'd just crossed the short distance to the front steps when Brigid's foot caught on the edge of a step. As she lifted her leg to get free, the car keys pushed the car alarm remote button in her pocket, setting it off. Brigid froze, panic setting in. Although her car was in Linc's driveway, it was still close enough that Rachele probably had heard it go off. Linc grabbed her hand and pulled her back around the corner of the house. Jett followed and they all hid, out of sight from the front door.

Moments later, the front door quietly opened and Rachele stepped out, a gun in her hand. She looked back and forth nervously. She took another step out into the darkness, hoping to see better. The backlighting coming from the house made it difficult for her to see.

"Drop the gun, Rachele," Linc's deep voice said as he stepped out from behind the corner of the house. "We know who you are, and we know you murdered Lucy. You can't pretend, anymore."

Rachele turned towards him and smirked. "You got that right. She had it coming to her for what she did to me. All those years stolen from me. And for what? It wasn't her money. It wasn't even her business. She should have just kept her nose out of it and let me do my thing. No harm, no foul. But she didn't. Instead, she ran to her brother and told him. Next thing I knew, my life was ruined. She got what she deserved.

"You can't stop me. I'll be long gone before you can even get in your car." Rachele couldn't see as well as Brigid and Linc could, even though her eyes had partially adjusted to the darkness. She faintly made out the partial outline of Linc's tall frame, but he blended into the bushes behind him. She aimed her gun and fired at Linc, her shot going wide. He dove for cover, heart racing.

Brigid knelt down by Jett and said, "Attack". Jett flew around the corner of the house as Rachele was stepping down from the porch, her suitcase in one hand and the gun in the other. Brigid heard Jett's four massive paws colliding with the ground as his large frame ran at full force towards the woman he hadn't liked from the time she'd arrived.

He launched himself at her, putting all of his one hundred thirty pounds into a flying leap. His body collided with hers in a violent crash, causing her to fall back onto the porch. Her gun and her suitcase were sent flying off the porch. Jett placed his front paws on her chest and held her down as Linc raced over, pointing his gun at her. Brigid joined him.

"Get this filthy mutt off of me!" Rachele screamed. She was wiggling and pushing against Jett with all the strength she had, but the dog never budged.

"I wouldn't test Jett, if I were you Rachele," Linc said as he continued to hold Rachele at gun point. "He's a trained attack dog, but that doesn't mean he won't decide he's tired of putting up with you and bite you. Brigid, call Deputy Davis. Tell him…" his voice was drowned out by the sound of approaching cars. A sheriff's car skidded to a stop in front of the house followed by two more squad cars. Deputy Davis rushed over to where Jett had Rachele pinned to the ground.

"Corey, how did you know?" Brigid asked.

"First, I need you to get yer' dog off her," Deputy Davis said, his gun drawn and trained on Rachele. *This had to be a first for me, getting' beat to an arrest by a dog,* he thought. *Don't matter, though. I'll take all the help I can get, four-legged or not.*

"Stand down," Linc said. Jett calmly left Rachele lying on the front porch and returned to Brigid's side where he flopped down on the ground. He almost seemed to smile proudly as he laid at her feet.

"I put everythin' together fairly quick after ya' hung up on me. Figured ya' was gonna' try to get her yerself'. It was jes' a hunch, but I was fairly certain y' was up to somethin'. I called two other deputies who were jes' leavin' the station to help me out. Figgered it was better to bring along some backup and not need it than to git out here by myself and find out I needed it."

He turned towards the two deputies who had joined him and pointed to Rachele. "Cuff her and read her rights to her, then get her to the station. I'm gonna' stick 'round here and search her room. Wanna' see if I can find any traces of chloroform. Need to make sure it's done by the book. Gonna' need a search warrant." He pulled out his cell phone. "Gimme' jes' a moment. Need to call Judge Landau, and we'll have one within the hour."

The deputies handcuffed Rachele and read her rights to her. "You can't prove I did anything wrong. I'm just here on vacation. Brigid's dog attacked me." Her voice began to rise and become shriller the closer she got to the squad car. "Oh no, no, no. I don't want to go back, please." She braced her legs, but the deputies continued to pull her toward the rear door of the squad car.

Corey stepped away to talk on the phone with the judge, leaving Brigid and Linc alone. "You okay?" Linc asked with a concerned look on his face.

"Yeah, I'm fine," she said as she smiled, feeling an imaginary weight beginning to lift off her shoulders. Knowing that her good friend's killer was in handcuffs was a relief. She only hoped it brought some peace to Rich when he finally heard the news. It wouldn't bring Lucy back, but at least her murderer had been caught. When Deputy Davis returned, she asked, "What's the warrant for? Why do you need it?"

"I want it 'cuz the coroner called me late today and said the preliminary tests showed that chloroform poisoning was the cause of Lucy's death, but she'd also been pepper sprayed. I wanna' search Rachele's room and see if I can find any evidence of one or the other." He shook his head. "Poor Lucy. Her last few minutes on Earth couldna' been too pleasant." The three of them were quiet as they watched Rachele being put in the back of a sheriff's car. "Judge don't live far from here. Said one of my deputies could pick up the search warrant in jes' a little bit."

"I can't believe I invited her here," murmured Brigid. "If I hadn't..." No matter how she rationalized it, the thought about her invitation kept bubbling up to the surface. How that one, innocent decision had ended up causing her friend her life.

"Brigid, you can't live the rest of your life thinking like that," Linc said, putting his arm around her. Even as he spoke he could only imagine how difficult it must be for her. He had a feeling it would be something she'd struggle with for a long time.

"Linc's right, Brigid. None of this is yer' fault. She woulda' found a way sooner or later," Deputy Davis said. They watched as the squad car pulled away, Lucy's murderer shackled in the back seat, the first part of her long journey to justice.

"You did it," grinned Linc. "You caught Lucy's killer."

Brigid smiled for the first time, "Well, I may have had a little help." She bumped his hip with hers and he laughed.

"Yeah, Jett's the real hero. Aren't you Jett?" he asked as he reached down and scratched the dog's head.

An hour later, one of Corey's deputies arrived at the house with the search warrant signed by Judge Landau and handed it to Corey. "This will make it legal for me to search the house," Corey said. "Mind showin' me her room?"

"Not at all." Brigid led the men into the house and down the hall to the guest bedroom.

The bed was made and everything looked as neat as when Rachele had arrived, except for the laptop on the bed.

"Looks like she forgot her laptop. We must have distracted her," Linc said with a trace of irony.

Deputy Davis carefully walked around the room, looking in every corner before opening the closet. On the top shelf he spotted a bottle and a rag. "What's this?" Corey said, sniffing it carefully. "Looks and smells like chloroform." He took a plastic evidence bag from his pocket and carefully placed the bottle and rag in it. "Something else's up here," he said, reaching farther back on the shelf. He pulled down a little spray bottle, unscrewed the lid, and sniffed it. "Smells like pepper spray, and it sure looks homemade." He put it in a separate plastic bag as evidence. "That her computer?" he asked.

"Yes, that's her laptop," Brigid said with a sigh. "She's such a good writer. I wonder if her book is on there?"

"Dunno, but I gotta' take it as evidence. If her book's on there, I assume her lawyer's gonna' ask that it be returned to her." He shrugged, "But who knows? She may not be of sound enough mind to even request it." Corey exhaled deeply. "Anyway, that's down the road. No need to worry about that right now."

An hour or so later, Linc and Brigid walked outside with Deputy Davis as he prepared to get into his squad car and leave. He turned to Linc and Brigid. "Can't thank ya' both enough for all yer' help. Rich'll be glad to know that at least one part of this nightmare is over. If ya' don't mind, I'd appreciate it if ya' both could come down to the station tomorrow and gimme' a statement. Don't worry about it tonight. Ya' both look just as tired as I feel. Let's meet up after we've had a bit of shut-eye, okay?"

Brigid and Linc both agreed as he turned around, got in his car, and left.

"Linc, thank you so much," Brigid said after Corey was gone. "If it wasn't for you, Jett and I could be dead. I shudder to think what that woman may have been capable of doing in order to cover her tracks."

"I don't think so, Brigid," Linc said. "You have much better instincts than you give yourself credit for. You knew something was wrong, and you were right." He pulled her close to him and hugged her. Brigid allowed herself to sink into his arms, feeling his warmth through his shirt. "By the way, I've decided I should spend the night. I don't think you should be alone after something like this."

Brigid felt herself tense. "Umm, Linc, I think it's too soon. I'll be fine. Jett's here with me."

Linc pulled back from her and laughed, "Brigid, it's not what you're thinking. I'll change the sheets and stay in the guest bedroom. Believe me, I'm not planning on doing anything else. I trust that will make you feel better."

"Much," she said as she relaxed. They continued to gaze into each other's eyes, barely able to see in the darkness. Slowly she stood on her tiptoes as Linc lowered his mouth to hers. Beneath the rising moon they shared a sweet yet intimate kiss.

EPILOGUE

Several months later, the day found Rich Jennings wiping down one of the counters in the kitchen at the B & B. He felt good working at the B & B, knowing that he was following in his family's footsteps. He was glad Henri had decided to sell the B & B to him. After Lucy's murder, Rich's heart just wasn't in law enforcement anymore. Getting up every day and putting on the uniform felt like a burden. All the fun and excitement had gone out of it.

Instead, he found a great deal of satisfaction, and yes, happiness, in keeping the B & B open and operating. He'd made a few changes and was planning to start doing more online marketing. Business had seemed to pick up, and he was proud of what he'd been able to accomplish in a rather short period of time.

Although Henri had done a good job running the B & B for a while after his wife's death, it didn't mean he wanted to keep doing it. When he mentioned to Rich he wanted to sell it, and Rich indicated he was interested in buying the B & B, it was a relief to him. He gave Rich a good deal on it, but he'd kept enough money so he could return to France. He'd lived in the United States long enough, and he wanted to go home, home to France, so he'd been eager to sell to Rich. Joelle Dubois quickly followed, leaving her escape artist kitty with her neighbor.

Rich stepped outside to get the daily newspaper from the porch. As he looked around for the orange wrapper that protected the paper from the weather, he noticed a sheriff's patrol car drive by. He lifted his hand and waved to Sheriff Corey Davis. Rich was glad Corey been able to take over the position from him when he'd resigned. Sheriff Davis' reputation had continued to grow and now there was talk that he might run for a higher office.

He wasn't sure what career path Corey would end up choosing, although they'd talked about it the other night when he'd stopped by to visit. Corey had confided in him that moving up the ranks had crossed his mind, but there was something about staying close to the people that really called to him. Rich just hoped Corey would choose wisely. He also wondered if Corey's English would improve if he did seek higher office.

Rich returned to the kitchen and pulled the newspaper out of its protective wrapper. On the front page was a big picture of Rachele Peters with the title "Peters Pleads Not Guilty." He began to skim through the article. He didn't really like reading about the details again, but he wanted to stay up to date on the trial.

Rachele had pled not guilty to the murder of Lucy Bertrand by reason of insanity. Whether her lawyer would be able to use her alleged lack of sanity as a means to keep her from spending the rest of her life behind bars remained to be seen. Rich thought the woman definitely had a few screws loose, but not to the extent that it would let her get away with murder. After all, he thought, if someone could write as well as she did, it would be hard to prove that person was insane. There was talk she'd end up behind bars for the rest of her life. As far as he was concerned, that wasn't long enough.

Rachele's writing career seemed to be up in the air as well. She'd grown in popularity as a writer, and those who followed the case were eagerly buying her books. Rich folded the paper and put it on the kitchen counter. He couldn't allow himself to think about any of it too much. Instead, he needed to direct his attention to keeping the B & B running smoothly.

Ouray Smith had approached Rich about the artifacts displayed in the B & B, but Rich proved to be just as stubborn as his sister in that he refused to return them to Ute Tribal Council. Ouray didn't care, though. He was determined to keep at it. If anything, maybe his perseverance would wear the man down. Ouray knew that preserving his Ute culture was going to be a tough job.

He was sure the reason he'd been chosen was because he had the strength and the willpower to keep going, even when it seemed like a lost cause. Ouray continued to harangue anyone he found who had Native American artifacts in their possession, Ute or otherwise. If they were local, he'd visit them personally. If they weren't, he'd call and email them relentlessly. He'd managed to get a few things returned to the tribes they had come from, but it was an uphill battle. That wouldn't stop him, though.

Farther away, Mike Loomis was shuffling around in state prison wearing a green jumpsuit. His days of skiing were behind him as he faced the prospect of serving the next few years in prison on drug charges. The guest at the ski lodge he'd tried to sell drugs to turned out to be an undercover narcotics officer. When they arrested Mike, he had meth and a pipe in his possession. That racked up additional charges, along with what they found when they searched his apartment. He knew he was going to be inside for a long time.

Jordan and Missy Blair continued to minister to the needs of their parishioners. They'd recently begun to host a Free Sunday Soup at the church and were considered to be assets to the little town of Cottonwood Springs. Missy has become known as the go-to person when anyone needs some help.

Missy happened to be attending a basketball game at the high school gym when there was a city-wide power failure during an early winter ice storm, which took everyone by surprise. She calmly organized everyone and when she'd taken care of the people at the gym, she began canvassing neighborhoods, helping those who were without heat get to the school where she'd been able to collect a supply of blankets and warm jackets. Once the power was back on, she was the last one to leave, making sure everyone was taken care of.

She's quite dedicated to the residents of Cottonwood Springs, and they return the feeling with warmth and admiration.

Fiona Garcia's book store continues to be a popular stop, not only for local residents but it's also become a "go to" place for tourists to visit when they're in Cottonwood Springs. Fiona has a vast knowledge of books and an uncanny ability to predict trends, but even more importantly, although less mentioned, is that she simply captivates people with her charming personality and astute insights into just about everything and everyone. She's taken Brandon and Brigid's advice and keeps a lot of what she thinks to herself, hard as it is at times. Almost everyone who visits Read It Again takes time to chat with her over a cup of coffee or tea.

Last, but certainly not least, are Brigid Barnes and Linc Olson. Since the night they caught Rachele, they've become more than just friends. Shared dinners, hiking trips in the mountains, or even just grocery shopping, are things they usually do together, and Jett is usually close by. Linc's grown a little concerned that Brigid may start a side business solving murders, since she had such good instincts with Lucy's. They've talked about their relationship but prefer not to put a label on things for now. They plan to take their time and see where things lead them.

On a recent night they were sitting on the couch in front of the fireplace enjoying the fire at Brigid's house, with Jett lying at their feet. "Thanks for dinner tonight," Linc said, lightly kissing her forehead. "It was delicious."

"Anytime," Brigid said with a smile, as she unfolded the daily newspaper. She took one look at the front page, folded it back up, and tossed it back on the table. "What do you think will happen to Rachele's book?" she asked.

"I don't know," Linc said. "It may just be collateral damage and get lost."

Brigid shook her head. "I'd hate to think of a really good story in a partially completed novel being lost. She really was an excellent writer, and her stories were so original." Her gaze drifted back to the window and the rain that had started. "I was thinking that if she's unable to finish it, I know several authors who could work with what she's written so far and make a bestseller out of it. That's what I always hope will happen for every one of my clients, that their book makes it onto the bestseller list," she said with a smile.

"I know nothing about bestsellers. That's your area, but let me tell you something, Lady, you're the best," Linc grinned as he pulled her close and wrapped a blanket around the two of them.

RECIPES

GOUGÈRES

Ingredients:
½ cup milk
½ cup water
8 tbsp. unsalted butter, cut into 4 pieces
¼ tsp. salt
1 cup all-purpose flour
5 jumbo eggs, room temperature
1 ½ cups coarsely grated Gruyere cheese (about 6 oz.)

Directions:
Position oven racks in 2 levels. Preheat oven to 425 degrees. Line 2 baking sheets with parchment paper. Bring milk, water, butter, and salt to a rapid boil in a heavy saucepan over high heat. Add flour all at once. Lower heat to medium low and stir briskly with a heavy whisk. The dough will come together and a light crust will form on the bottom of the pan. Keep stirring, for an additional 1 – 2 minutes to dry the dough. It should be very smooth.

Turn the dough into a heavy-duty mixer with a paddle attachment. Let dough rest for 1 – 2 minutes, then blend in the eggs, one at a time. Make sure each egg is fully incorporated before adding the next egg and don't be concerned if the dough separates. By the time the last egg goes in, the dough will come back together. Beat in the cheese.

For each gougère, spoon 1 tbsp. of the dough onto the prepared baking sheet, leaving a 2" space between them. Place the backing sheets in the oven and immediately turn the oven temp down to 375 degrees.

Bake for 11 minutes, then rotate the pans from front to back and top to bottom. (Ovens vary, so these are approximate times.) Continue baking until the gougères are golden, firm and puffed, approximately 9 more minutes. Serve warm or transfer to a cooling rack and serve at room temperature.

NOTE: Traditionally gougères are served with champagne or kir when a guest came to someone's home in France.

GARBANZO BEAN SALAD

Ingredients:
3 lemons
2 tsp. olive oil
1 tbsp. minced garlic
1 cucumber, peeled, seeded, and chopped into 1" pieces
½ red onion, chopped into 1" pieces
1 cup cherry tomatoes, halved
1 can garbanzo beans, drained
2 tbsp. parsley, finely chopped
Salt and pepper to taste

Directions:
Squeeze the juice of the 3 lemons into serving bowl. Add olive oil and minced garlic. Add cucumber, red onion, cherry tomatoes, and garbanzo beans. Stir to combine. Season with salt and pepper to taste. Garnish with parsley. Refrigerate for one hour prior to serving.

EASIEST CHOCOLATE PEANUT BUTTER COOKIES EVER

Ingredients:

2 cans (16 oz. each) chocolate fudge frosting
1 egg
1 cup chunky peanut butter
1 ½ cups all-purpose flour
¼ cup granulated sugar

Directions:

Preheat oven to 375 degrees. Set aside 1 can plus 1/3 cup frosting. In a large bowl, combine egg, peanut butter, and remaining frosting. Stir in flour until moist. Drop rounded tablespoons of the dough 2" apart on greased baking sheets. Flatten cookies with a fork dipped in sugar. Bake for 8-11 minutes or until set. Remove to wire racks. Cool completely. Spread with remaining frosting. Enjoy!

SO EASY CHICKEN WITH 40 CLOVES OF GARLIC

Ingredients:

1 whole chicken, cut into 8 pieces (I have used quarters as well)
½ cup + 2 tbsp. olive oil
10 sprigs fresh thyme
40 cloves of garlic, paper skin removed
Salt and pepper
Aluminum foil

Directions:

Preheat oven to 350 degrees. Season chicken with salt and pepper. Toss with 2 tablespoons of olive oil and brown on both sides in a wide ovenproof frying pan over high heat. Remove from heat. Add remaining olive oil, thyme, and garlic cloves. Cover with aluminum foil and bake for 1 ½ hours.

Remove chicken from oven. Let rest for 5 to 10 minutes and serve. Enjoy!

PASTA WITH FRESH BASIL PESTO SAUCE

Ingredients:
2 cups fresh basil leaves, packed
½ cup freshly grated Parmesan cheese (about 2 oz.)
½ cup extra virgin olive oil
1/3 cup pine nuts
3 cloves of garlic, paper cover removed and minced
¼ tsp. salt, or more to taste
1/8 tsp. freshly grated black pepper, or more to taste
Pasta of choice
Food processor

Directions:
Prepare pasta according to package directions. Five minutes before pasta is ready, place basil and pine nuts in a food processor bowl and pulse several times. Add the garlic and cheese. Pulse several more times, then scrape down the sides of the food processor with a rubber spatula.

With the food processor running, slowly add the olive oil in a small steady stream. Stop two to three times to scrape down the sides of the processor. Stir in salt and pepper. Toss with pasta. Serve and enjoy!

SURPRISE!

PUBLISHING 11/3/18
MURDER AND THE MUSEUM

BOOK SEVEN OF
THE HIGH DESERT COZY MYSTERY SERIES
http://getBook.at/MATM

All Camille wanted to do was build a museum in the desert. Too bad someone didn't agree and she was murdered. But was it for the land or her millions?

That property was prime desert land. A lot of people wanted it. Tortoise Lady, the Mafia investors, and the Indian tribe. And Camille's son and daughter-in-law wanted her millions. Makes for a lot of motives and suspects.

Detective Jeff is busy with two other investigations, and definitely needs his wife's help. Good thing Marty has a psychic sister and a psychic dog to help!

This is the seventh book in the popular High Desert Cozy Mystery Series by two-time USA Today Bestselling Author, Dianne Harman.

Open your smartphone, point and shoot at the QR code below. You will be taken to Amazon where you can pre-order 'Murder and the Museum'.

(Download the QR code app onto your smartphone from the iTunes or Google Play store in order to read the QR code below.)

ABOUT THE AUTHOR

USA TODAY bestselling author and seven-time Amazon All Star Author, Dianne Harman, draws her stories and characters from a diverse business and personal background. She owned a national antique and art appraisal business for many years, left that industry, and opened two yoga centers where she taught and certified yoga instructors. She's traveled extensively throughout the world and loves nothing more than cooking, playing backgammon with her husband, Tom, and throwing a ball for their dog, Kelly.

Being a dog lover and having attended numerous cooking schools, she couldn't resist writing about food and dogs which led to her cozy mystery series. Her award series include:

Cedar Bay Cozy Mystery Series

Cedar Bay Cozy Mystery Series - Boxed Set

Liz Lucas Cozy Mystery Series

Liz Lucas Cozy Mystery Series - Boxed Set

High Desert Cozy Mystery Series

High Desert Cozy Mystery Series - Boxed Set

Northwest Cozy Mystery Series

Northwest Cozy Mystery Series - Boxed Set

Midwest Cozy Mystery Series

Midwest Cozy Mystery Series - Boxed Set

Jack Trout Cozy Mystery Series

Coyote Series

Midlife Journey Series
Alexis

Red Zero Series

Black Dots Series

Cottonwood Springs Mystery Series

Newsletter
If you would like to be notified of her latest releases please go to www.dianneharman.com and sign up for her newsletter.
Website: www.dianneharman.com,
Blog: www.dianneharman.com/blog **Email:** dianne@dianneharman.com

Made in the USA
Monee, IL
28 August 2023

41771086R00100